Doreen's specialty is canines. . .not men.

"Would you mind holding him while I go outside and see what happened to my leash?"

"Sure." Doreen studied the excited dog and decided he couldn't really be so badly misbehaved all the time. She watched Edwin walk toward the door, checking back over his shoulder many times, watching her hold his dog while he stepped around the mess. As soon as he disappeared through the door, Doreen let the dog go. She stepped in front of him, squatted, and looked him straight in the eye, resting her hand on his forehead to make sure she had his attention before she spoke again.

"Bulldozer, sit," she commanded in a stern tone.

The dog sat. Doreen smiled.

Bulldozer whimpered, but did not move, even with his master out of sight.

Doreen grinned triumphantly at Bill, who was scanning the strewn contents of the display rack and his entire selection of scratching posts on the floor.

"I think there's hope for the dog," she said, optimistically.

Bill's gaze was now on Edwin, who had reappeared and now stood barely outside the doorway. Edwin bent at the waist to pick something up off the ground, straightened as he examined it, fumbled with it, and dropped it, then hunkered down to search once again for whatever it was.

Bill sighed. "Yes, but is there hope for his owner?"

GAIL SATTLER lives near Vancouver, British Columbia, with her husband and three children. *Walking the Dog* is her first published novel, and her own Standard Schnauzer was a major inspiration for the story.

Walking
the Dog

Gail Sattler

Heartsong Presents

A note from the author:

I love to hear from my readers! You may correspond with me by writing:

> **Gail Sattler**
> **Author Relations**
> **PO Box 719**
> **Uhrichsville, OH 44683**

ISBN 1-57748-310-3

WALKING THE DOG

Cover illustration by Victoria Lisi and Julius.

PRINTED IN THE U.S.A.

one

Doreen blew the silent whistle and waited. For thirty seconds, the only sound was the wind rustling through the treetops in the summer breeze.

Then they came. In the distance, she could hear the crescendo of barking, accompanied by the snap of twigs under the rushing of anxious paws. The startled flight of birds from the branches overhead signaled their imminent arrival.

The thin whippet broke into the clearing first, followed by the muscular Doberman, then the midsized dogs. After a few minutes, the toy poodle appeared and finally, scrambling for all he was worth, came the Yorkie.

"Sit," Doreen commanded with a downward motion of her palm in the air.

All sixteen dogs sat immediately. Instant quiet.

Doreen smiled. This had not been an easy accomplishment. Pulling the name sheet out of the back pocket of her worn jeans, she commanded the dogs one by one to come, to heel, then jump into the back of her van, where she deposited them into numbered travel kennels, securing all her charges before she continued on her way.

As far as businesses went, this one had been a minimal investment. While the work was easy, the advertising had been far more difficult than she had anticipated. Despite notices and business cards posted in all the local veterinarians' offices, poodle parlors, and whatever pet stores she could convince to display her flyers, all leads for more business had dried up. She had posted some flyers at the local supermarkets recently and on her church bulletin board, hoping for the best.

In order to turn a profit, she needed four more dogs. If she could get to twenty, she would be able to pay off her small loan and make a comfortable living.

She tossed the leashes in the box on the seat beside her and checked her appearance in the rearview mirror. Not that the dogs cared what she looked like, but she never knew when she would run into a potential customer.

The brisk wind left her face flushed, emphasizing the freckles on her cheeks and nose. Grinning at her reflection, she picked a twig out of her chestnut hair, a souvenir from being knocked down playing fetch with all sixteen dogs at once. Her clear, blue eyes sparkled. This was the best job she had ever had.

Doreen knew her small business, Walking The Dog, would be a success; she could feel it in her bones.

Her friends all thought she was crazy, but as she began to attract more inquiries and, finally, serious customers, their teasing turned to fascination and respect. Still, they kidded her about being "the president and founder" of Walking The Dog, Ltd., not to mention the only employee.

Doreen stopped the van to close the large chain-link gate behind her, then continued on her way to take the dogs back to their respective homes.

One by one, each was delivered, and by supper time, she was back home. Before allowing herself the luxury of a break or a bite to eat, she first checked her kennels, and restocked the supply cupboard with a new supply of dog biscuits. She was not above using bribery.

When everything was ready for the next day, she returned to her house to prepare supper. Running around with a bunch of dogs all afternoon was hard work. At least some days it might be considered hard. She grinned.

On her way through the living room, the flashing light of the answering machine attracted her attention. She waited anxiously for the tape to rewind, hoping the message was a potential new customer rather than someone to whom she owed money. After distributing some rather expensive new flyers, she had hoped to have received at least a few calls by now.

"Hello?" a male voice asked hesitantly, then paused. She sympathized with the caller's reluctance to leave a message. She hated answering machines herself, but she couldn't afford to miss a single call. "Is this the place that looks after dogs? My name is Frank Chutney, and I'd like you to call me. I have some questions."

Unable to control her excitement, Doreen let out an excited whoop, then needed to replay the message to get the phone number. If this man became another client, she would be almost at her goal. She made a mental note to ask him where he got her phone number.

She dialed immediately, but instead of reaching him, she was greeted by a taped message. In the background, she heard a yappy little bark, most likely another terrier. Doreen left a message, ending with a joke about playing telephone tag, and informed him that she would be home all evening awaiting his call.

As she hung up the phone, her gaze drifted to Gretchen, waiting patiently beside her bowl, tail wagging.

"Well, old girl," she said as she playfully ruffled the dog's ears, "I hope we'll have one more playmate for you soon."

Gretchen was a good dog. Even though her beard was constantly dirty, and her boundless schnauzer energy was sometimes hard to match, Doreen loved and appreciated her companion. It was an autumn hike with Gretchen that started Doreen thinking about Walking The Dog as a career.

Who would have thought she could make a living exercising dogs? Of course, there was more to it than merely walking them. She had to pick them up, all sixteen—maybe seventeen, soon—exercise them, give them a snack and some water, then let them run free until it was time to deliver them back home to greet their owners when they returned from work.

The phone rang as she lifted her first bite of mashed potatoes. Quickly, Doreen turned down the television.

"Hello, Walking The Dog," she replied, trying to sound businesslike. She kept a wary eye on Gretchen, who was stalking her abandoned supper plate over on the coffee table.

"Hi, this is Frank. I phoned earlier. Evelyn Forthwright gave me your name. I might need your services. Do you have any vacancies?"

Yes! A customer! Doreen pulled one fist through the air in a gesture of triumph, then cleared her throat, trying to contain her excitement.

"Yes, I do," she said calmly. "My name is Doreen McCullough, and I'm the owner. What information do you need?"

"Everything," Frank replied.

She recited her rehearsed speech with all the details, and before she knew it, she had dog number seventeen signed up.

She glanced anxiously at the clock as she rescued her dinner from under Gretchen's hungry and hopeful gaze. She needed another kennel and leash to accommodate her newest client, who would be starting the following morning. She had half an hour to get to the pet store before Bill went home.

Doreen gulped down a few bites of lumpy, cold potatoes, dumped the rest in the sink, grabbed her keys, and ran out the door. "Okay, Gretchen. You can come."

❧

Edwin checked his wristwatch as his car screeched to a halt in the driveway. Traffic had been terrible, causing him to be half an hour later than usual getting home. Frustrated from sitting in bumper-to-bumper traffic, he gritted his teeth at the thought of his poor dog locked in the house all day.

He turned the key in the lock and eased the front door open. Dozer shot past him, making a beeline for the large tree in the middle of the front lawn. Edwin chuckled and heaved a sigh of relief. He was as grateful as the poor dog that he had made it home in time.

He wished a neighborhood kid could let Dozer out at lunchtime, but he knew that a schnauzer could sometimes be a difficult dog for a young kid to handle. The neighborhood teenagers, who wouldn't be alarmed by Dozer's exuberant exit, stayed at school for lunch. Sometimes the dog's boundless energy and enthusiasm caught Edwin himself off guard. Bulldozer had turned out to be a very appropriate name.

"Come on, Dozer," Edwin called over his shoulder. "Get back in the house, boy!"

"Eddie! Can I have a word with you?" a feeble but stern female voice called to him from the end of his driveway.

Edwin cringed. Only one person, other than his grandmother, called him Eddie: old Mrs. Primline, the neighbor from across the street. He knew what was coming, and it was too late to hide. How could such a sweet, little old lady make a twenty-five-year-old man feel like a naughty little boy?

Turning around in slow motion, Edwin forced a smile on his tired face. "Good day, Mrs. Primline. How are you this fine evening?"

"Don't give me that," his neighbor chastised him sharply, wagging her finger in the air as she spoke. "That dog of yours howled for hours after you left again! The poor thing is in pain. Why haven't you called the vet or something? Can't you do something for that animal?"

Trying to keep a straight face, Edwin remembered the words of a friend's little boy regarding Dozer's vocal talents. "The dog isn't in pain, Mrs. Primline, he's just very sad to see me leave in the morning."

"That animal's howling rattles my windows. I could swear he was being tortured."

Edwin forced himself to smile at his scowling neighbor. "Schnauzers do howl, Mrs. Primline. I'm just one of the lucky owners whose dog howls better than others. Maybe if I gave him voice lessons, he could focus his pitch into a more soothing melody."

Edwin laughed at his own joke. Mrs. Primline did not. Not that he expected her to, but today he couldn't help himself. It had been a bad day at work and he wanted nothing more than to put his feet up and catch the game on TV. So far, he had been unable to convince her that the dog's howling, while no doubt disturbing, was relatively normal.

"It's got to be a toothache. I know how bad that feels, that's why I've got dentures," the old lady continued to complain. "Have that dog's teeth checked!"

Her complaining was soon going to make him howl

right along with Dozer. "Sure thing, Mrs. Primline. I'll do that. Good night."

To his relief, she turned around in a huff, stomped off down the driveway, across the street, and into her house, closing the door with a heavy slam.

In her own way, the old lady was a good neighbor. Most other people would probably call the police, but Mrs. Primline's primary concern was for the welfare of the animal.

Edwin opened the front door all the way and stepped into the house. Dozer trotted along gaily behind him, oblivious to the discord on his behalf.

On his way to the kitchen, Edwin grabbed the remote control for the television, flipped on the game, and shuffled into the kitchen to search the fridge for anything edible that wasn't green. Leftover pizza beckoned from the lower shelf. He heated it in the microwave, grabbed a soda, and sat down on the couch.

Dozer pranced in front of the television, his pink tongue lolling out, then sat, cocked his head, and cast his doleful eyes on Edwin. Edwin had just taken his first bite when he noticed Dozer's big, brown eyes staring at him. He dropped the lukewarm pizza on the plate and sighed as he turned off the television.

"All right, I'll take you for a walk." It was just as well. After sitting most of the day and then being cramped up in the car, a walk would do him good.

"Can't you wait until I'm finished eating?" He grumbled and gulped down the remaining pizza. How did that stupid dog learn to get under his skin like that? "Next time, I'll just get a goldfish."

Edwin left the dirty plate on the coffee table, then headed to the door with Dozer following admiringly behind. "You win, come on. We're out of treats, so let's go for a walk to the pet store."

At the word "walk," Bulldozer lived up to his name. Bounding down the stairs in his haste to get to the door, he bumped into Edwin, almost knocking him over, then tripped on the last stair, slid on the linoleum, and crashed into the door for a grand finale.

By the time Edwin made it down the stairs, Dozer was jumping up and down and whining loudly.

"I know, I know," Edwin mumbled as he sat on the stairs to put on his sneakers. He attached the leash to Dozer's collar, smiling at his dog's enthusiasm. "I wish I had the energy you do at the end of the day."

After carefully locking up, the two of them made their way at a comfortable pace on the three-mile walk to the pet store.

Upon their arrival, Edwin tied Dozer's leash to the bicycle rack, pushed the door open, and paused. He grinned as he noticed a "No Pets Allowed" sign. "Hey, Dozer. They're happy to have you as a customer, but you're not welcome in their store."

Inside, he picked up a variety of dog treats and a rawhide chew, and waited his turn at the counter. It was mere minutes before closing time, but there was another customer at the register. When he caught a glimpse of the young lady ahead of him, he was more than happy to wait for her.

She was average height, but that was the only average thing about her. Shoulder length brown hair framed a lovely face with a sprinkling of freckles across her cheeks and the bridge of her nose. Her blue eyes shone, highlighting the most charming smile he had ever seen. The woman smiled and laughed as she spoke to the proprietor. *Wow,*

Edwin thought to himself. *She can smile like that at me anytime.*

Doreen laughed as Bill finished his story. Even though she saw him every Sunday, their casual greetings in the crowd at church couldn't compare to talking with him one-on-one at his store.

She appreciated that Bill stayed open late. He couldn't match the wholesale prices of the giant pet store across town, but he always gave her a hefty discount, and the personal service could not be matched. Their families had been friends for years, and Bill had been a close friend of her uncle's before he died.

Bill had always been her biggest fan and was the first person to actively encourage her to start her own business. He always had a funny story to tell and, around Bill, she didn't feel self-conscious about her boisterous laugh.

Out of the corner of her eye, Doreen noticed that the young man who had come in a few minutes before was ready with his purchase, so she stepped aside to let him pay, wiping the tears of laughter from her eyes. She was in no rush, and wanted to stay and chat with Bill a little longer. After the store closed, she would most likely end up at his house for coffee and to visit with his wife. Gretchen would wait obediently in the van.

As she waved Edwin toward the counter, she couldn't help but notice that he was very attractive. He looked a bit older than her twenty-two years, but he fit the profile of tall, dark, and handsome. His dark brown hair had a tinge of red, and he had the deepest brown eyes she had ever seen. Most people might say he needed a haircut, but Doreen liked it.

Caught staring, Doreen's gaze shifted to the floor. She felt the rising heat in her cheeks. It appeared that he had been evaluating her, as well. Cautiously, she raised her eyes again.

Doreen froze as their eyes met. How embarrassing. She'd never seen him before in her life.

Edwin stood transfixed. Vaguely, in the background, the old cash register clunked and clattered as the proprietor rang up his small purchase. "This everything?" the man asked politely.

Edwin blinked, then turned his head to face the man. "Uh, yes," he answered as he reached to the back pocket of his jeans for his wallet. He laid a few bills and his wallet on the counter while he dug in his pocket for some loose change.

As he fumbled for the coins, he glanced as casually as he could manage at Doreen. Their eyes locked once again.

Caught completely off guard, Edwin continued to stare until she blinked and looked shyly down at the floor again.

What in the world was he doing, making eyes with her like that? He tried to contain his blush, but he couldn't look away.

A loud bark from outside, accompanied by grating and scraping noises, broke the spell. Dozer, standing on his hind legs and stretched full-length, leaned against the glass door, whining. He barked again when he saw Edwin look at him, then frantically scratched the glass door with his front paws.

"Dozer!" Edwin gasped. "How did you get loose?" Edwin dropped his change on the counter and raced through the store to retrieve his dog before disaster struck. Dozer possessed absolutely no street sense, and was likely to run into the street and get hit by a car!

The second Edwin opened the door, Dozer lived up to his name again. Dodging Edwin's hand, he made a run for it. Edwin took a frantic swipe at his collar, but Dozer eluded him and dashed into the store.

Edwin's stomach clenched as he watched Dozer bound up the aisle, knocking over a row of scratching posts for cats, a display of food and water dishes, and a few other assorted items on his way. Then, to Edwin's horror, Dozer headed straight for Doreen and jumped up on her, his paws landing abruptly in her midsection, sending her sprawling backwards into a rack of stuffed toy mice. As if in slow motion, her hands flailed, little fuzzy rodents flew into the air, and everything—dog, Doreen, and dozens of mice—crashed to the floor.

Doreen winced as she landed. Edwin could have died.

Jumping over the mess his dog had made, Edwin ran as fast as his legs would carry him through the store. Dozer was dancing excited circles around Doreen. She scrambled to her feet before Edwin could help her up.

"I'm so sorry!" he exclaimed, wishing he could melt through the cracks in the floor. "Are you hurt?"

Doreen sucked in a deep breath, fighting the urge to rub her tender backside in front of the two men. "It's not that bad, I'll be fine."

Bending down to calm Dozer, Edwin continued to hold the unruly dog while he extended his other hand to Doreen. "I'm really sorry. I'm Edwin Olson, and this idiot is aptly named Bulldozer. Are you sure you're okay? Please, I'd like to make this up to you."

Looking at Edwin through slightly blurry eyes, Doreen held her breath. Judging from his red face and the tremor in his hand as she returned his handshake, the poor guy felt awful.

"It's okay, really, I'll be fine," she said tightly, trying to smile. "My name is Doreen McCullough. I think your dog is just being friendly. He probably smells the other dogs on me."

Edwin remained in a crouched position. To dispel his embarrassment, Doreen tried to think of something to say.

She cleared her throat. "Nice schnauzer you've got there. I've got one, too. I know how energetic they can be."

Edwin blinked and stared at her. "You've got a standard schnauzer? They're not a common breed." The redness in his face had started to subside, but the heat and color returned when he glanced down the aisle at the mess Dozer had made. "I thought I had him tied securely outside. I guess I was wrong." He felt like an idiot hunched over holding Dozer's collar, but he was too nervous to trust the dog to stay calmly at his side without being held. Caught in a spot, he forced himself to face the proprietor, chancing his wrath for the mess. "I'm really sorry about this. I'll take care of everything as soon as I take care of the dog." He turned to Doreen. "Would you mind holding him while I go outside and see what happened to my leash?"

"Sure." Doreen studied the excited dog and decided he couldn't really be so badly misbehaved all the time. She watched Edwin walk toward the door, checking back over his shoulder many times, watching her hold his dog while he stepped around the mess. As soon as he disappeared through the door, Doreen let the dog go. She stepped in front of him, squatted, and looked him straight in the eye, resting her hand on his forehead to make sure she had his attention before she spoke again.

"Bulldozer, sit," she commanded in a stern tone.

The dog sat. Doreen smiled.

Bulldozer whimpered, but did not move, even with his master out of sight.

Doreen grinned triumphantly at Bill, who was scanning

the strewn contents of the display rack and his entire selection of scratching posts on the floor.

"I think there's hope for this dog," she said, optimistically.

Bill's gaze was now on Edwin, who had reappeared and now stood barely outside the doorway. Edwin bent at the waist to pick something up off the ground, straightened as he examined it, fumbled with it, and dropped it, then hunkered down to search once again for whatever it was.

Bill sighed. "Yes, but is there hope for his owner?"

two

Edwin found the leash still firmly tied to the bike rack, and the reason that Dozer was not attached to it. The ring that was supposed to hold the tags and fasten the leash to the collar lay bent and broken on the ground next to the leash. Edwin picked it up, then tried to twist it back into shape with his fingers. When the jagged metal jabbed his palm, he flinched and dropped it. He picked it up again, then stared at the broken piece of metal in his hand. That dog had more strength than he thought to break something he couldn't even bend. At least he was in the right place to buy a new collar. He picked up the scattered dog tags, flipped the broken piece into a garbage bin, and shoved Dozer's tags in his pocket as he opened the door with his other hand.

On his way through the store, he slowly and carefully picked up the merchandise Dozer had knocked over, taking great care to rearrange everything in neat rows. He righted the cat-scratch display, carefully replaced all the dog toys that had fallen onto the floor, and stacked everything else neatly where it belonged.

ঌ

Bill and Doreen watched from a distance. Doreen felt torn between helping poor Edwin and dutifully standing beside his dog, knowing that once she moved, his dog would follow. So far, Bulldozer remained still, but she knew he wouldn't last much longer.

Bill smiled and whispered to her, "You know, Doreen,

part of me wants to go help the poor boy, and part of me is enjoying watching him put everything back so neatly. I think it's straighter and more organized than it was before his dog knocked everything down. Maybe I should hire the boy. Or the dog."

Doreen blushed, because she was enjoying watching him, but for a different reason. "Bill!" she admonished him in a stage whisper, "I hardly think he's a boy!"

"I know," Bill whispered back, leaning forward over the counter, "but no matter how old you get, you'll always be Marie's little girl to me."

With all the fuzzy mice and last rubber bone neatly back in place, Edwin returned to the counter. He grinned at Doreen and Bill, and scowled at his dog, who remained in front of Doreen, as good as gold.

"You don't deserve this, you rotten animal!" he grumbled, then smiled again at Doreen.

Doreen couldn't help but giggle. He was trying so hard. Edwin turned back to face her. "Doreen—may I call you Doreen? I meant it when I said I wanted to make this up to you. Does it hurt?"

"It's not that bad," she said, smiling despite the numbness of her backside. She would simply sit cautiously, or remain standing as much as possible. "It's okay, really."

Edwin refused to take no for an answer. Impressed by her forgiving demeanor, he became more determined to get to know her. "Can I at least buy you a coffee then?"

"Buy me a coffee?" she parroted, then looked at Bill, who cleared his throat and turned around to straighten a display that wasn't crooked. "Well, I don't know. . ."

Edwin wanted to convince her that his intentions were honorable, or at least most of his intentions were honorable. "Please, I have an idea. Why don't you give me your phone number, and I'll call you in a few days after you've thought about it. Nothing serious, just coffee, and if you don't want to meet me, then I'll never bother you again, no questions asked."

Doreen tilted her head slightly to study him. She usually socialized only with the young men from her church, whom she had met before or whose families she knew. Normally, she would never consent to go out with a stranger, but she felt herself weakening. She pulled one of her business cards from the small display on Bill's counter and handed it to him.

Edwin blinked as he studied the printed card. It featured a cartoon picture of an unhappy dog with its face pressed against a window, with "Walking The Dog, Ltd." in bold type at the top, and "Day Care for Dogs" in small letters underneath.

"Day care for dogs?" he asked incredulously. He stared at the name Doreen McCullough and the phone number at the bottom. "This is you? Is this for real?"

Her eyes widened, and Edwin immediately regretted his response, which had not come out as he had intended.

"Yes, that's my card."

Edwin glared at Dozer, still sitting in front of Doreen, the longest he had ever seen his dog sit still. "It appears you have a way with dogs," he tried to put on his most charming smile, hoping he hadn't blown it with his lack of finesse.

To his relief, she smiled back. "Well, I do handle dogs for a living, but in addition to that, I have a schnauzer, too, remember."

He flashed his best lady-killer smile. "Do you find your dog a bit difficult to handle at times?"

"Not really. My Gretchen is just as bounding with energy,

but I will say that she behaves better than your Bulldozer does."

Edwin lost his smile. He blushed, hating the rush of heat to his face. "I, uh, don't think that's all that difficult. . ." He swished his foot on the floor to buy himself some time to think. Most dogs were better behaved than his, and he knew it. "Maybe I could use your professional services, but in the meantime, the offer of going out for coffee is still valid." Rather than look at her again for fear of being turned down, he bent to scratch Dozer's ear.

Doreen wondered what he was thinking. She pressed on. "It's getting late. I'd better go." She pulled her credit card out of her purse to pay for her new purchases so she could let Bill close out the register.

Fitting his new collar around Dozer's neck, Edwin clipped the leash on, and picked up the bag of dog treats. He flicked her business card with a little snap, and tucked it into his wallet. "You'll be hearing from me." He winked as he called back to her, turned, and led Dozer out of the store.

Whether or not he became a new client, Doreen anticipated going out for coffee with the man with the energetic dog. At the click of the door closing, Doreen turned to Bill. "Well?" she asked.

Bill grinned back at her. "Well, what?"

Doreen rested her hands on her hips. "Well, what do you think?"

"He seems like a nice boy." Bill's eyes twinkled and the crinkles at the corners of his eyes became more pronounced with his teasing smile. "Overmatched, but harmless enough."

"Does he come here often? Do you know anything about him? I'm not sure if I should go out with him, because I've never met him before."

"What do you need to know?" Bill asked, his eyes not losing their teasing glimmer. "He spoils his dog rotten, he feels bad about you getting knocked over, and he pays cash."

Doreen frowned. "Bill! Get serious!"

Bill shrugged his shoulders. "I don't know him either, kid. If you go out with him to a regular public place, though, he'll probably be fine. You might even have a little fun. Besides, if he started having you look after his dog, you'd be seeing him in private anyway, so what's the difference? You trust your customers at some point, don't you?"

"Well," Doreen drawled thoughtfully. "I guess so."

"It's up to you. He seems okay to me."

Doreen shrugged as she pictured Edwin's playful grin in the back of her mind. The way their eyes had met was almost embarrassing, but he did seem like a respectable guy.

"Who knows? He probably won't even call. He only felt bad that his dog knocked me over. He'll forget about me before the day is over."

"Maybe." Bill shrugged his shoulders. "Maybe not."

❧

The next evening, Doreen sighed with relief as she delivered the last dog to its home. Her first day with Frank Chutney's dog had turned out more hectic than anticipated. Chipper had not behaved as well as promised. Next time, before she took on another dog, she would be sure it was adequately trained.

Back when she had had only a few dogs to care for, one or two running away from the group didn't matter. Now that the ranks had swelled in number, one rowdy dog could be the difference between order and chaos.

Because Chipper was a small dog, it was an easy matter to pick him up when he didn't listen and carry him back to his assigned kennel in the back of the van. However, it was not a procedure she wanted to do often.

She left a short note on Frank's kitchen table, encouraging him to practice obedience lessons with his dog, and to call her if he needed help. Unless his master practiced basic obedience commands, Chipper would require more attention than Doreen had time for. Still, she could not afford to lose a paying customer.

As Doreen drove home, her thoughts drifted back to Bill's words. If Frank Chutney, her newest customer, requested a private consultation to learn basic commands to use with his dog, she would schedule an appointment for him on her property without giving it much thought. Therefore, she should have no qualms about meeting Edwin Olson, whom she also didn't know, in a public restaurant. The only difference was that one was a client and one was only a potential client. But what could be safer than a public place?

Doreen shrugged her shoulders as she turned into her driveway. Chances are he wouldn't call anyway.

When Doreen walked into the house Gretchen began to run excited circles around her, waiting impatiently for supper to be served. Doreen threw her a cracker and began to search the cupboard, hoping for something interesting but quick. Finally, she settled for macaroni and cheese with a fresh carrot on the side. She had no energy for anything more elaborate.

With her less-than-gourmet supper in hand, Doreen headed into the living room to watch her favorite program. On her way to the couch, she noticed the light flashing on her answering machine. She put her plate down on the coffee table, pressed the button and waited for it to rewind, hoping for another new client.

A male voice she didn't recognize stammered, "Hello? Doreen? It's me, Edwin Olson, uh, remember me? I'm the one with the, um, unruly schnauzer, uh, you know, at the pet store? Um, anyway, ah. . .man, I hate your answering machine. No, I didn't mean that, I hate them all. I, um, oh, forget it. I feel like I'm talking to myself. Anyway, how'd you like to, ah, go out for something to eat or something? No, that came out wrong. I mean, you wanna go out with me some time? I mean, oh, never mind. I'll call back later." A fumbling noise was followed by a loud bang that sounded like he dropped the phone, and then a click as he hung up.

Doreen bit her bottom lip. Did the man take lessons from his dog? She rewound the tape, wondering if he would have the nerve to call back. Would he realize that he hadn't left his number? After his bold introduction yesterday, his stumbling message confused Doreen. "Wait a second. Why am I even thinking about this guy?"

Dismissing her thoughts, Doreen relaxed comfortably on the couch and switched to her program already in progress. The phone rang just as she took her first bite of macaroni. Doreen answered with her mouth full and one eye still on her show.

"Walking The Dog," she mumbled, hoping it wasn't obvious she was chewing.

"Doreen? It's me, Edwin."

Doreen choked on her supper. Coughing and hacking, she tried to regain a professional tone. "Oh, Edwin." She swallowed, trying not to make any rude noises into the phone. "I got your message earlier. How are you?" She raised one hand to her blushing cheek, grateful for the distance between them on the phone.

Edwin gritted his teeth. He had sounded like a bumbling idiot earlier, and he knew it. There was nothing he hated more than talking to a machine, especially when he was already nervous and hadn't anticipated leaving a message. He usually didn't fall apart quite so badly, and he hoped to salvage a modicum of dignity so she would still consider going out with him.

"I thought I'd call and see how you were feeling, if you were okay, and if you would join me for coffee or something this evening." He tried not to gasp for air as he rushed everything he wanted to say into one breath. It hadn't been that long since he asked a woman out, but he hadn't been so jumpy since high school. He tried to stifle the fear that she might try to avoid him, now that she didn't have to look him in the eye when she told him to get lost. While part of him knew a woman might be wary about meeting someone she didn't know, another part of him was kicking himself for giving her an easy way to turn him down. A little voice in the back of his brain told him to shut up before he blew it completely.

Doreen tried not to giggle. The poor man sounded as nervous as she felt. Although it was getting late, she decided to give him the benefit of the doubt. "I guess I can meet you somewhere for coffee. Where do you want to go?" She tried to sound more casual than her nervous stomach indicated.

"You pick."

"Well," Doreen drawled, "tell me where you live, and we can pick something halfway." She forced herself to relax her tight grip on the phone, then shoved one hand in her pocket.

"Why don't you tell me where you live. I'll just swing by. After all, isn't the male supposed to escort the female?"

Doreen fumbled with the phone. "Look, it's late. I'd prefer to meet you halfway. Besides, my house is kind of hard to find in the dark."

He gave what sounded like a nervous laugh. "Oh. Well, as long as you're not trying to avoid me, I guess we can do that."

Doreen unclenched the fist in her pocket, and switched to running her fingers through her hair. "So, can we just meet somewhere?" She didn't want to sound timid or afraid, but she didn't want to bruise his ego either.

"Of course, of course. I live by the new mall," Edwin stammered.

"How about the Cafe House, then?"

"Okay, good. I know from experience that they have great chocolate cake."

Doreen didn't know if her stomach could handle chocolate cake, but a cup of coffee would be fine. "What time is good for you?" Doreen untangled her fingers from her hair to check her wristwatch. "I was just about to eat my supper, but I could be there in forty-five minutes."

Edwin glanced quickly at his watch. "Sure. Sounds good. See you soon." He heaved a sigh as he hung up the phone, and wiped his sweaty palms on his jeans. He was ready to leave now, and he had a feeling the next half hour could be the longest thirty minutes of his life. He decided to walk Dozer around the block a few times to use the pent-up energy he had stored. *I gotta take it slow, though; I don't want to be all sweaty.*

≈

Doreen hung up the phone with a shaking hand, unable to believe she had agreed to go out with a man she had just met—at the pet store, of all places. Before now, she had only gone out with mutual acquaintances, men whose background she already knew and where there was already some relationship—not that she intended to have a relationship with Edwin. They were simply meeting for coffee, and then she would probably never see him again.

She turned to retrieve her supper, left unattended on the coffee table for the duration of her phone call. Her hand froze in mid-reach. The macaroni was gone, only the carrot remained, and Gretchen, who was supposedly well trained, was nowhere to be seen.

Doreen's stomach rumbled as she stomped into the kitchen to make herself a peanut butter sandwich.

As Doreen pulled into the Cafe House parking lot, her doubts began to catch up with her. Edwin had seemed like a nice enough young man when she met him at Bill's store, and he was cute over the phone, but what was he really like? And even though they had met just the day before, she started to worry that she wouldn't be able to remember what he looked like. Images of the classic tall, dark, and handsome male, with emphasis on the *handsome,* flashed through her mind. Then she changed her mind, Switching the emphasis to *tall*. Next, she thought of his dark, dark brown eyes.

She dashed the images from her mind as she pulled into a parking space. Daydreaming was pointless. Beyond this one meeting, she had no intention of seeing him again. With one last check of her hair and lipstick in the rearview mirror, she slid out of her seat, locked the van, sucked in a deep breath, and headed toward the Cafe House.

Edwin sat at a table near the window, watching. The second Doreen's van turned into the parking lot, he jumped to his feet. The huge, lumbering vehicle was unmistakable. The same cute caricature of a lonely dog that was on her business card was painted larger than life on the side of the van. It was a moving billboard, with WALKING THE DOG and Doreen's phone number in large, bold, Day-Glo letters on the side. He hoped they would never have to meet secretly anywhere.

When the door of the van opened, Edwin crossed his arms over his chest and waited. His little walk with Dozer had helped keep him busy for half an hour, but it did nothing to quell the nervous energy that he barely managed to control. When he had first arrived, he had taken up residence in front of the dessert counter and worried as he watched the chocolate cakes being sliced and served. After a while, the hostess politely showed him to the table beside the window and seated him with a complimentary coffee, promising she would reserve two pieces of their specialty double chocolate cake for him and his guest.

Gathering all the casual charm he could muster, he now sauntered to the door, holding it open as Doreen approached. He smiled, doing his best to look calm, cool, and collected, and wondered if he had her fooled.

Doreen smiled back and nodded politely as Edwin held the door open for her. He appeared confident and completely unruffled; meanwhile, her stomach was fluttering like a schoolgirl's.

"Been waiting long?" she asked as the door closed behind her.

"Nah." Edwin shook his head, but Doreen detected a slight hesitation in his voice. "Just long enough to check out the cake."

three

Edwin led Doreen directly to the table. Before she had a chance to speak, one of the waitresses placed a steaming cup of coffee and a thick slab of double Dutch fudge cake in front of her. She winked at Edwin as she handed him his cake before returning to her duties behind the counter. Edwin blushed and shrugged his shoulders. "I already told them what we wanted."

As Doreen bent to slide her purse under her chair, Edwin's eyes remained glued to her every move. Cute, and attractive in her own way, he now decided, Doreen was not drop-dead gorgeous or anything like that. While she had a certain composure about her, she didn't ooze poise or charm or anything particularly compelling, but there was something different about her, different than other women he dated. Not that he dated many, but he intended to date this one. He tried to put his finger on what it was, but couldn't.

His thoughts were drawn back to the present as Doreen straightened in her chair, positioned herself comfortably, then smiled at him. Face to face with her across the table, he stared into her sparkling blue eyes, opened his mouth to speak, but his mind went blank.

"I trust Bulldozer won't be making an entrance?" Doreen playfully peeked over one shoulder toward the door, then looked back at him.

Edwin did his best to appear chagrined, sipping his coffee to collect his thoughts. "No, I took Dozer for a walk before I came, and left him at home sleeping. I only call him Bulldozer when I give him a lecture for doing something bad. You know, like when your mother talks to you and uses everything, including your middle name, and you know you've done something really bad? I don't know why I talk to him like that, but I guess most pet owners do. I once had a friend that talked to his rabbit, and he swore the dumb thing answered."

Doreen smiled and nodded as she started to eat her cake. "I've been known to talk to Gretchen at length, myself. Lots of people talk to their pets. That's because they're good listeners." She pushed her plate to the side, leaned over the table in a conspiratorial manner, motioning to him to do the same.

Entranced, Edwin leaned forward, meeting her halfway across the table. Her voice lowered to a husky whisper, making Edwin lean even closer. She glanced from side to side before sharing her secret. "I've occasionally caught Bill talking to the fish in the back of his store." She sat, still leaning over, eyes twinkling, expecting a response. Then she winked.

Edwin's heart contracted almost painfully, his eyes widened, and his stomach clenched as he stared into Doreen's face. He knew from that moment on he was lost. Had she suddenly gotten prettier? She absolutely glowed.

He gulped to clear his head, trying to pick up the conversation where they left off, mimicking her sideways glances. "Do they answer back?" he asked in a stage whisper. Even though Pet Stuff was a fair distance from home, he often shopped there because he got a kick out of the old guy behind the counter. If Doreen knew the man, maybe he would have to go in more often.

Both of them straightened in their chairs simultaneously

to take slow, cautious sips of the steamy hot coffee. Their gazes locked. Edwin held the cup in front of his mouth with both hands, grateful it was ceramic and not the disposable paper variety, which was the only thing saving him from crushing it and sloshing hot coffee down the front of his shirt. "Tell me about yourself."

She clasped her cup on top of the table, the smile never leaving her face. "What do you want to know? I just might hold the world's most exciting career. I do day care for dogs for a living."

Edwin sucked in a deep breath, deciding not to comment further. "Well," he drawled, "I meant stuff like how old are you? What do you do in your spare time? Got a serious boyfriend? Married? That kind of stuff."

Her face paled, her lips parted, closed, then she swallowed before she spoke. "No, I'm not married and I don't have a serious boyfriend. And I don't really have any spare time."

He couldn't help but grin. "Great. I'm not married, and I don't have a serious boyfriend either. So when do you want to go out with me?"

Doreen sputtered into her coffee, then grabbed her napkin, holding it to her mouth as she coughed into it.

"Are you okay?" Edwin asked, wondering if he should pat her on the back or call the waitress for a glass of water.

Doreen waved her hand in front of her face. "Fine, fine," she rasped, then cleared her throat. "And what do you mean, go out with you? We are out."

"This isn't going out," he countered. "This is business. Besides apologizing for my dumb dog, I wanted to ask about your services. I feel guilty leaving Dozer alone all day, and your card got me thinking. Got a sales pitch for me?" Edwin sat back in the chair and folded his arms across his chest, encouraging her to go on.

"A sales pitch?" she croaked.

"Hit me with your best shot."

Doreen stared at him, but he only stared back. He was apparently serious. "Well, I'll pick up your dog, exercise him, and bring him back home. For a fee."

Edwin's lower lip quivered in a poor attempt to stifle a chuckle. "Exercise him? You mean take him for a walk? You really do that, just like the name on your card? Walk dogs?" He broke into a broad grin. "What do you do, go to the nearest park, let them. . .you know. . .then get out the old pooper-scooper, and take them home again?"

Doreen bristled. She clenched her teeth rather than say something she would surely regret. She had heard this typical response before, only this time she liked it even less, and no one else had ever made such a production out of it.

Edwin wiped his eyes, then his smile instantly dropped when he looked up. "Uh, did I say something wrong? You're not saying anything."

Battle lines had been drawn. Before she could stop herself, Doreen began a verbal tirade. "There's a lot more to it than simply taking a dog for a walk. First of all, I'm bonded because I have access to all my client's houses, and I'm responsible for locking up and resetting any alarms. I have a special large, air-conditioned van to hold up to twenty dogs, each of which has to have a kennel and leash. And I can't just run twenty dogs around the local park. I bring them to my two-acre property, which is completely fenced and secure. I'm also fully qualified to teach dog obedience. There's more to this than simply taking a dog for a walk around the block." She sat back in her chair and folded her arms, waiting for him to make a smart comeback.

He looked appropriately contrite. "Oops. I guess I never thought about it that way. Sorry, I didn't mean to offend you." Hesitantly, he held his hand out over the table, in the offer of a handshake. "Still friends?"

Still friends? She had never been friends with him in the first place. However, in view of his repentance, Doreen regretted her brusque response. Edwin was far from the first person unable to take her business seriously, nor was he likely to be the last. Even though she tried not to take it personally when people laughed, it still stung.

Unable to ignore his friendly gesture, Doreen reached out to take his hand, gave it a timid squeeze, and quickly let go, folding her hands in her lap. "No, I'm the one who should apologize. I shouldn't be so sensitive; after all, it's not like no one's ever laughed before. I must admit, it's not a very mainline profession." Doreen smiled tightly and reached under her chair for her purse. "If you want to think about it, I'll give you my brochure. It has a brief description of my services, and my requirements before I accept a dog. After all, I have to worry about my own safety, too."

He quirked one eyebrow, all traces of laughter gone. "Oh? Have you ever been bit?"

She hesitated, then continued to sort through her purse, remembering the instance well. "No, but I came close once. I refused to take on a couple of pit bulls, not only because they almost bit me, but I have to consider the safety of the other dogs. It was too bad, because I really could have used the money." Finally reaching the pile of brochures at the bottom of her purse, she slid one across the table. "And I didn't like the owner."

Thinking this would be a good time to shut up, Edwin scanned the information. "You got your prices on here? Oh, never mind, I see them." He turned it over to read a list of various charges for other services on the back page. "Hmm. . .day care, veterinary visits, obedience, accident notification." He stopped reading. "Accident notification?"

Doreen blushed. "You know, *accidents*. . ."

"Uh, I'm afraid I don't. . ."

"Um, most of the time, people hire me not so much out of guilt for leaving their dog alone, but because the dog, uh, has difficulty being locked inside for so long, and um, messes in the house. I call to let them know what to expect, and where."

"Oh. Accidents." After she had gotten so angry with his reaction earlier, Edwin didn't know if he was allowed to laugh, but if she kept gawking at him, he wasn't going to be able to contain himself much longer.

Doreen looked down at her hands, unable to face him. "It's not my favorite part of the job, but it happens." She raised her eyes to meet his. "And thank you for not laughing."

One corner of Edwin's mouth twitched, as if he was trying very hard to keep himself from laughing again, no doubt afraid of her reaction. She smiled at his admirable attempt, which destroyed all his noble efforts. Both of them started to giggle, clearing the heavy atmosphere that had developed between them.

Edwin's eyes twinkled. "You still haven't answered my question."

"Question?" She couldn't remember him asking anything specific.

"Yeah. I asked when you were going to go out with me."

A blush spread from cheek to cheek and down her neck. Keeping her head down, she picked at the piece of cake, hoping to avoid answering.

"So, you busy tomorrow?"

"Yes, I am."

"How about Friday, then?"

"Sorry, I'm busy Friday evening."

"Saturday for lunch?"

"Sorry, I'm busy all day."

"Oh," he mumbled, then lowered his head. He toyed with the last bit of cake on his plate, then laid the fork down and pushed the plate away. "I'll probably call you sometime about Dozer, then."

A pang of remorse stabbed her. She hadn't meant to hurt his feelings, she really had obligations. "But I'm not busy Saturday night," she added quickly, reaching out to rest her fingers on the back of his hand. As soon as her fingers brushed the fine hairs, she pulled her hand back, realizing what she had done.

His head jerked up as he spread his fingers wide, then drew his hand back, rubbing where she had touched with the fingers of his other hand. "Want to go to dinner, then?"

Anticipation heightened his handsome features, making her heart quicken. What had she done? But since no serious commitment was implied in accompanying him for dinner, she decided to go ahead. "I should be free about six. Is that too late?"

"Not at all. The timing is perfect. We can avoid the dinner rush. Let's say I pick you up at, say, seven?" He turned the brochure over, then pulled a pen out of his pocket. "Where in the world is Cumberland Road?"

"I'd rather meet you at the restaurant. Either that, or I could go to your house."

The pen hovered in midair for a few seconds before he put it down. First she refused to allow him to pick her up, claiming her house was difficult to find in the dark. He wondered what her excuse could be this time. "Why don't you want me to see your house?" he asked. Did she have a boyfriend or husband after all?

"I don't care if you see my house. It's just that I live out a ways and I'll already be in town; in fact, not far from here. It seems silly to have you go all the way to get me when I'll already be close by and all dressed to go. Or is there a reason you don't want me to pick you up?"

It didn't do wonders for his ego to have a woman pick him up for their first official date, but if that's what it took, Edwin decided it was worth it. Of course he would insist on doing the driving. "Whatever," he mumbled.

Doreen smiled her response, and continued to nibble on the cake while Edwin wondered about her plans for tomorrow and Friday night, and then again Saturday afternoon. Was she going out with someone else? Despite her denial of having a serious boyfriend, the thought of any type of boyfriend, however casual, did not sit well with him. And he noticed she wasn't volunteering any information on her plans, or explaining why she would be all dressed up and ready to go out. How could he find out without looking foolish, or worse, jealous?

"So," he started, his mind racing as he tried to find the right words, "is your other, uh, engagement, going to let you go in time for a seven o'clock dinner?"

"Engagement? Well, it starts at four-thirty, so it will probably be over no later than six."

"Over?" No date he had ever been on had been timed by a punch clock.

"Sure. Most brides are late, but usually by no more than fifteen minutes." Doreen finished the last of the coffee in her cup and dabbed her mouth with her napkin.

"Bride? You're going to a four-thirty wedding, and everyone is going home before six? What kind of boring wedding is that?"

"Oh, I'm not going to the reception. I don't even know them."

"Then why are you going to the ceremony?"

"It's part of the job."

"Part of the job?" he echoed. *I thought she baby-sat for dogs.*

"I play piano for my church, including weddings. I've been to dozens of weddings over the past few years. It's a good thing I don't cry at weddings, or I'd be in trouble."

"You play piano for weddings? You mean you get paid for that?"

Except for the staff, Doreen and Edwin were the last patrons at a table. She bent to retrieve her purse, checked over her shoulder at the wall clock, then back to him. "Yes, I get paid for weddings because they're on the weekend, but I do Sunday mornings as a volunteer."

"Sunday mornings? Like, for church? Hymns and stuff?"

"Of course. Edwin, I think they want to close. We should leave."

He remembered the little old nun who played the organ at the church his family went to when he was growing up. She was awful, and the huge pipe organ blasted so loud it rattled the windows. He couldn't imagine Doreen playing like that.

She stood first, so Edwin picked his keys up off the table, and accompanied her through the parking lot. As they walked to her van, he tried to picture Doreen playing the wedding march, hoping she played better than Sister Mary. The thought of Sister Mary and her hard line with the children in her charge almost made him shudder, despite the warmth of the evening air. Of course, he hadn't seen Sister Mary or the inside of a church any more often than he had to.

"Good night Edwin, thanks for the cake and coffee. I had a nice time." Doreen stood beside the open door of her van, her hands clasped in front of her, waiting for his response.

Edwin blinked and shook his head a couple of times. "You're welcome. See you Saturday, and I'll call you."

"Sure." Doreen hopped up into her seat and closed the door. She started the engine, backed out, and drove away, leaving Edwin standing fixed in the same place.

Before she turned the corner, she checked the rearview mirror to see if Edwin had moved. She had felt oddly hurt to see the change in his expression and demeanor when she told him that she volunteered as a church pianist. Did it matter to him that she was a Christian, and that she actively participated in her church? And if he wasn't a Christian, should she really be going out with him?

As she got closer to home, Doreen realized that he had not given her his address or offered directions to his house, nor had he given her his phone number.

He had said he would call her, but from the look on his face, she wondered if he would. It was probably just as well. Nevertheless, she felt a twinge of disappointment.

four

Doreen's fingers flew over the keyboard as she finished the last strains of Mendelssohn's triumphant exiting "Wedding March" from *A Midsummer Night's Dream*. The new bride and groom assembled in the parking lot with all their guests, exchanging greetings and congratulations. Echoes of cheers and laughter from the happy crowd outside drifted through the empty church building. Nothing filled her with joy like a summer wedding.

Gathering up her sheets of music, Doreen tucked everything neatly into a file folder, ready for the next wedding, closed up the piano, and stored the folder in the bench.

Between her busy activities and obligations, she had not made it home until late every evening this week, and had not spoken to Edwin since they met a few days ago, but he had left a message on her answering machine Friday night with his address, phone number, and directions to his house. Thankfully, this time he was much more coherent than the first cryptic message he left.

Careful to avoid anyone she knew, Doreen slipped out the back door and carefully unfolded the paper with the directions to Edwin's house. As it turned out, the church was only five minutes from his house, which meant she was going to be half an hour early. She hoped he was ready.

⁂

Edwin rifled irritably through his closet, trying to decide what to wear. What would Doreen be wearing? If she was playing for a wedding, how would she be dressed? He shuddered inwardly as strains of the "Wedding March" drifted through his mind. Never in a million years.

He thought of Sister Mary and her nun's habit, compared the image to Doreen as he had last seen her in jeans and a sweatshirt, and shook his head. Even though Doreen would not be wearing a nun's habit, she would probably still wear something subtle and old-fashioned, somber background material. Plain colored and dull. He didn't own anything that would complement dull.

He pushed aside another shirt, then changed his mind and pulled it off the hanger anyway. It was his favorite shirt, and he was going to wear it. A nice cheerful blue, it matched the great silk tie with Bugs Bunny on it that would cheer up any dark and drab outfit or duo.

With the tie tucked underneath his collar, Edwin craned his neck to start fastening the buttons of his shirt. The doorbell rang. Dozer jumped off the bed and bounded to the front door, barking all the way on his mad run through the hall and down the stairs. His nails clicked and scraped on the linoleum as he stumbled on the slick surface, followed by the usual thump as he slid into the door. *One day that dog will learn to slow down.*

Edwin checked his watch, running through a mental checklist of who it could be. Doreen wasn't due for half an hour. Did he owe the paperboy money already? Grumbling under his breath, he grabbed his wallet from atop the dresser and jogged to the door. Dozer jumped up and down, pawing the front door, barking with great vigor. After a few mad scrambles, Edwin finally managed to get a grip on his collar, pulled him back with one hand, and opened the door with the other.

"Hey, you little brat, aren't you kinda early?" he chided

the boy as the door opened. Every time the kid came to collect, Edwin enjoyed giving him a rough time, just as the kid enjoyed teasing him back. "Didn't I just. . . ?" Edwin gasped and blushed ten shades of red. "Doreen!"

He squeezed Dozer's collar tighter as the dog continued to bark and pull. He blinked twice, unable to believe his eyes. Instead of background basic black, Doreen wore a slim-fitting pink dress, showing all her feminine curves to good advantage. Her skirt fluttered in the breeze against slender but shapely legs, ending with a pretty pair of pink high-heeled shoes the same color as the dress. He trailed his gaze up the length of her and back to her face, but before he could say anything, his breath caught.

The other times he had seen her, her hair had been loose, with untidy waves barely brushing her shoulders. Today, her ordinary brown hair had been transformed into a graceful swept-up style, loosely pinned with a few wisps cascading down, framing her face in such a way that it took every bit of self control he possessed not to run his fingers in it, brush it back, and kiss those cute little freckles across the bridge of her nose. Either that, or kiss off the luscious cranberry lipstick that adorned her soft, pouty lips. He tightened his grip on Dozer, gulped, and stared.

Doreen smiled in greeting, but was met with silence. Edwin remained bent at the waist, holding Dozer down as the dog struggled to free himself, barking nonstop. Instead of inviting her in, he stood in the doorway, red-faced with his mouth hanging open, not moving, staring up at her, his eyes wide and bright.

At first, Dozer's attempts to appear ferocious held her attention, but a flash of color caught her eye. The unknotted tie, draped loosely around Edwin's neck, swayed in the opening of his unbuttoned shirt, drawing her gaze to the center of his chest. She probably could have counted the hairs there on one hand, but what really drew her attention was the slight tensing and flexing of his muscles as he struggled to hold back the straining dog.

Far from a muscle-bound beachbum, he appeared . . .endearingly average. The thought occurred to her that she was probably in better condition than he was. At least she ran and exercised with the dogs every day. Until now, the question of what he did for a living had not occurred to her. Obviously it was not a physical job.

She averted her gaze, staring purposely straight into his eyes. "Did you. . .uh," she stammered. "It's been a long time since I've been called a brat, but you're right, I guess I am kind of early. Shall I come back later?" She backed up a step, hugging her purse in front of her, prepared to return to her van parked on the street.

"No!" he exclaimed, his face developing a deeper shade of red. "Uh, no," he mumbled in a quieter tone. "Sorry, I didn't mean that. I thought you were the paperboy. You look. . .nice. Please come in."

Edwin muttered something under his breath that Doreen couldn't understand and pulled the dog backward. As soon as she stepped inside, he pushed the dog roughly to the side, then clutched his shirt closed in front of him. "I'm not quite ready, as if you couldn't tell."

The second Edwin stepped away, Dozer moved into action, but this time, she was prepared. Using her knee, she blocked him from jumping up onto her dress. "Down!" she commanded, but Dozer appeared to be preparing himself to jump again. Dropping her purse on the floor, she grabbed him by the scruff of the neck and pushed down, forcing him to be still. The dog whined, then sat quietly.

Edwin whistled between his teeth. "Not bad. I guess I'm

going to have to train him a little better." Edwin answered her firm scowl with a silly grin.

"That wouldn't be a bad idea." She let the dog go, never breaking eye contact with him. Dozer hunched down, flopped onto the floor, then rolled over onto his back with all four feet sticking up in the air. She waved her hand over him. "Look at his submissive posture. This dog is just begging to be trained."

Edwin looked down at his dog, then back at her, and shuffled his feet. "He may look kind of pathetic, but he's really a good dog." He looked down at his handful of shirt, released it, then used his hand to smooth out the small wrinkle he had made. "Excuse me, why don't you have a seat in the living room, and I'll be right back."

When she moved to kick off her shoes, Dozer wagged his tail, returned upright, then followed as Edwin directed her to the couch to wait. He flipped the television on and handed her the remote control, then disappeared up the stairs. Dozer padded over to her and laid his head in her lap. Gently, she petted him as he rubbed his snout on her knee.

&

"Sorry about that," Edwin said quietly as he reentered the living room, this time fully presentable in a tweed sport coat and a conservative, solid-color tie. With his hair combed and neatly in place, he looked much older than he had on their previous meetings.

"Please, don't apologize. I didn't know what else to do with that extra half an hour, so I took my chances and decided to be early." *Wasn't he wearing a Bugs Bunny tie before?*

He paused in front of the mirror over the fireplace to straighten the knot on his tie. "You look very nice. I didn't expect you to be wearing something so, uh, bright."

"Bright?" Doreen looked down to evaluate the color of her dress. She had not considered this dress bright. If he didn't like the color, then she supposed it was a good thing she had not worn her first choice, which was a vivid purple. "I was at a wedding, not a funeral. What did you think I was going to wear?"

"Never mind." Edwin glanced at his watch. "It's a little early for our reservation. Can I get you a drink before we go?"

"Sure. A glass of water would be great."

Water? *That wasn't quite what I had in mind.* Edwin sauntered into the kitchen and returned with a glass of cold ice water.

"Nice wedding?" he asked as she accepted the glass from him.

Doreen smiled and nodded politely. "Yes. It was a couple from my church getting married this time, but sometimes it's people who would never step foot in a church except for the day they get married, wanting to seal their vows before God. I especially like that."

"I suppose." Edwin shrugged his shoulders and looked out the window at her van. He didn't want to go out to a high-class establishment in that monstrosity. The large van itself wasn't bad, but the picture of the dog on the side and the vivid, foot-high lettering had to go. How could he ask her tactfully to let him drive, and take his car?

"Do you go to church, Edwin?"

"Huh? Yeah, sometimes." *Maybe I could hide her keys. Does she have them already tucked away in her purse? Maybe if I hid her purse…*

Her voice interrupted his little scheme. "Sometimes?" she asked.

"I usually go to church for midnight mass on Christmas

Eve with my parents. And of course, Mother's Day. Every once in a while I'll go if there's something special happening." If he couldn't steal her keys, maybe he could let the air out of one of her tires. He had a compressor in the garage, and could reinflate it easily for her to go home.

"Something special?"

Special? What were they talking about again? "Oh, if a friend's baby is christened, you know, that kind of stuff." The van was parked on the street. *How can I get to it in time to do anything?*

"Maybe we should go, Edwin."

"Sure." He glanced furtively at her purse, which she now held firmly in her hands. He sighed in defeat, then tried to decide which was more important: the pleasure of her company or their mode of transportation. His plan was to have a pleasant evening with Doreen. He would make the best of it. He tried to make himself feel better by reminding himself that her van was air-conditioned, while his car was not.

After he locked the front door, he turned to walk down the sidewalk to Doreen's van, but stopped dead in his tracks when he saw her waiting in his driveway beside the passenger door of his car.

She wiggled the door handle. "It's locked."

He sagged in relief, and tried to contain his smile. He knew he should feel ashamed of himself for all his planning and scheming, but to admit to it would only leave a bad impression.

Fishing his keys back out of his pocket, he unlocked the door and opened it with a flourish. As the door swung wide, a wave of heat blasted out from the car, the slight updraft causing the stray wisps of hair he'd been dying to touch to float for a second. He rolled the window down for her as she sat down, then closed the door.

The fan blew at the same time as he started the engine, blasting another wave of hot air in their faces. Doreen fanned herself with her hand, then turned to him with a sheepish expression. "I guess I'm not used to this; the van is air-conditioned."

Edwin bit his tongue, clamped his lips together, and nodded. "I guess I forgot to open up the car this afternoon. It will cool off quickly as soon as we start moving." He backed out of the driveway, and once they were moving forward, accelerated quickly to create enough of a breeze to cool the car's interior to a more comfortable temperature.

"I leave the air-conditioning on for the dogs between stops. I can't leave the animals in a closed vehicle, because each pickup can take up to ten minutes. They would suffocate. And I must admit, it sure is nice to get back into the cool van."

He smiled, feeling even more ashamed of himself. "I'll bet."

"You didn't tell me where we're going. Am I dressed appropriately?"

She was dressed more than appropriately. "It's a surprise. I wanted to impress you."

Her eyebrow twitched at the information he hadn't meant to divulge, but thankfully, she didn't comment.

The line at the entrance to the restaurant seemed daunting, making Edwin grateful for his foresight in making a reservation.

When Doreen requested coffee instead of a cocktail, Edwin frowned, and discontentedly ordered the same. As soon as the waiter was out of earshot, he lowered his menu to the table as Doreen quietly read hers, looking absolutely adorable as she tried to make up her mind. Despite the fact that the evening had only just begun, he wanted to ask her out again. "You could have ordered something stronger than coffee, you know. And I hope you're not going to embarrass me by ordering the cheapest thing on the menu."

She shook her head, but didn't look up as she used her finger to trace something down the page. "Oh, I don't drink. Don't take it personally." She lowered the menu, folded her hands on it, then grinned at him. "But if it'll make you feel better, I'll order the most expensive thing on the menu, and request extra garlic bread, heavy on the garlic."

He couldn't for the life of him remember what he was going to say. "You don't have to go that far," he mumbled and picked up his menu again, hiding his face behind it. Upon the waiter's return, he picked the first thing that looked good, and settled back in his chair.

"You must have had a busy week. I don't know how many times I phoned, but you were never home. I finally gave up, but I hated to leave a message on an answering machine to invite a lady on a date."

"Oh, it was just a normal week, except for the wedding rehearsal, and the actual ceremony today."

"At least you can relax and sleep in tomorrow."

"Tomorrow is Sunday."

"I know. The day to sleep in."

"I have to get up earlier on Sunday than any other day, because I play for both services."

"Oh. Then can you relax when you get home?"

"Well, usually I go out for lunch after church, and by the time I get home, its almost supper time."

"You can relax after supper?" Judging from the expression on her face, he doubted it.

"No, I go back to church to play for the evening service."

Did he dare ask? "You're probably busy Sunday night too, aren't you?"

Doreen smiled as he stared at her in utter disbelief.

"Sunday night, I check all my supplies and kennels and things to get ready for Monday's dog run."

Edwin lifted his hands in the air for a brief second. "I give up!"

ઈ

Edwin watched Doreen's big, ugly van round the corner and disappear as he stood in the driveway. He couldn't remember the last time he had had such a good time with a woman. In fact, if he were honest with himself, he'd never had such a good time with a woman.

As the night had progressed, he had found himself loosening up more and more, and by the end of dinner, he had completely opened up. Toward the end of the evening, he'd even broken down and confessed his fear that she was going to drive them to the restaurant in her big, ugly van. Not only had she sympathized and agreed that the van was ugly, but she had laughed at his schemes to make it temporarily inoperable. He still couldn't believe it. She'd laughed. The only downside to the evening was her evasive maneuvers when he tried to ask her out for a second date. That was, until they got back to his house.

After a very pleasant dinner, Doreen had agreed to come in for coffee, and after the usual greeting at the door, he had not given Dozer a second thought. That had been his mistake.

Instead of throwing the dog outside, he had been so enchanted with Doreen that he had forgotten about Dozer and the doting way the dog had become attached to her. While no one was watching, his idiot dog reappeared with a soggy wet rawhide chew, thunked his front paws on her knees as she sat on the couch, then dropped the slimy hulk onto Doreen's lap, leaving a disgusting wet mark on her nice dress.

At the time, Edwin thought he would die, but Doreen surprised him by laughing as she threw Dozer's treasure into the backyard, pointedly closing the door after him when he ran outside to fetch it. Then she had continued their conversation as if nothing had happened.

They had sat and talked until almost midnight, until she reminded him that she had to get up early in the morning, and had to leave. And tomorrow she was busy from morning to nightfall. Sunday promised to be a long and lonely day.

ک

Doreen turned the key in the lock to open her front door. Without caring where they landed, Doreen kicked off her shoes as soon as she stepped inside, and let a huge yawn escape. She was pleasantly surprised to have thoroughly enjoyed herself with Edwin. "Man, I am just dog tired." She couldn't even smile at her own joke, Gretchen did not seem to appreciate it, either. After wearing high heels all day, her feet ached. She wiggled her stiff toes and slipped her feet into her soft, fuzzy slippers.

Today had been a busy day, topping off a busy week. Despite the fact that she really didn't know Edwin, she couldn't remember the last time she had enjoyed herself so much. She fought it, but she couldn't help but respond to Edwin's sense of humor. Even when he wasn't outright joking, she had to smile at his playful attitude. Even though he didn't have a serious bone in his whole body, she still enjoyed his company.

Nevertheless, she hadn't wanted to discover that they shared many common interests, and liked the same books and movies. All evening, she had deftly avoided pointed hints to see her again socially. But just when she thought he got the message, he asked if she would add Bulldozer to her client list.

Even though she needed more dogs in order to become profitable, she turned him down. She refused to accept any dog that wasn't adequately trained. At least Edwin hadn't tried to bluff his way through that one, but when he started to beg, she couldn't take it anymore.

The final straw had come when Dozer dropped his soggy rawhide chew in her lap. Edwin had been so embarrassed that she caved in and agreed to help him. She didn't know how he did it, but he got her to agree to make arrangements for the following weekend to begin some basic dog training.

This time, no matter what he said or did, Doreen intended to keep things strictly business. She may have been rooked into spending an afternoon with him, but she would not go out for dinner with him again. She would not meet him for coffee in the evening, and if his dog did not respond adequately to instruction, she would never see him again.

She smiled, knowing schnauzers trained easily, then scowled at where her thoughts were leading. Her future plans did not include Edwin Olson.

Knowing she would be rising early, Doreen piled her music books beside the door in preparation for the first Sunday morning service, and went to bed.

five

Taking a deep breath, Doreen closed her eyes and rested one hand on her stomach, trying to calm her nervous energy. Today was scheduled to be strictly a business visit. She planned to work on some basic obedience training for Edwin's dog, nothing more.

Fluffing her hair, she took another deep breath and straightened her blouse with her hands. She probably didn't look any different than she looked two minutes ago, the last time she checked herself in the mirror.

In the distance, a car bumped up her gravel driveway, followed by an echoing silence as the hum of the engine ceased.

He had arrived.

Doreen blinked and shook her head as she peeked through the curtains. Dust wafted around the car in a cloud, but Edwin did not get out. At first, she assumed Edwin was waiting for the dust to clear, but soon she was able to see Edwin attempting to snap the leash on Dozer. As usual, Dozer was not cooperating.

The dog jumped soundly in Edwin's lap, making Doreen wince in sympathy. After a number of failed attempts to catch him, Dozer bounced back and forth between the front and rear seats, making it impossible for Edwin to get a grip on him.

Doreen figured that it would be easier if Edwin simply opened the door to let the dog out, but she knew Edwin wanted to make a good impression by bringing his dog to the door obediently on the leash. She hoped he would swallow his pride and give up, because judging from his progress, or lack thereof, he was losing the battle. Badly. Dog one, owner zero.

Finally, Edwin managed to snap the leash onto the collar. The car door opened. Doreen stifled a smile as Dozer bolted out, pulling Edwin with a powerful lurch strong enough to jerk his head back. Dog two, owner zero.

So as not to betray her presence, Doreen gently eased the curtains shut and waited for Edwin to ring the doorbell. Gretchen ran across the room, barking and jumping against the door before Edwin came within ten feet of it. On the outside, Doreen heard Dozer barking in response, accompanied by frantic but unheeded commands to sit, stay, heel, lie down, and finally, to shut up. Dog three, owner zero.

Doreen waited patiently behind the closed door, but soon began to wonder why he had not rung the doorbell. Placing her hand on the doorknob, Doreen looked at Gretchen. Had Gretchen barked so much she had not heard it?

"Sit," commanded Doreen quietly but firmly, her hand remaining on the doorknob. Gretchen sat in silence, waiting for the door to be opened, her tail wagging so fast and furious that the whole dog shook, but she obediently sat as commanded.

Doreen quietly opened the door to see Dozer sitting, and Edwin hunkered down with his back to the door, gently steadying the dog by the snout with one hand, the other holding up the dog's shaggy eyebrows as he stared Dozer sternly in the face, unaware that she was standing behind them.

"Listen, you large-nosed idiot," he explained softly and slowly, as if the dog were capable of understanding, "when you meet a lady, you're supposed to be cool and calm and collected, show her you're suave and sophisticated. Show her you have style. Impress her."

"Oh, I'm impressed, all right," she snickered. Dog four, owner definitely still zero.

Startled, Edwin stood abruptly and faced her, his face beet red. "Oh, I, uh, didn't hear you. We were just having a little chat."

"I see," Doreen said with a half smirk. "And how much of that little chat do you think he's going to obey?"

Edwin shrugged his shoulders. He'd been caught. "None, I'd think." He looked down to see Doreen's dog sitting quietly and obediently at her side. The only sign of excitement was a rapidly wagging stump of a tail. "I don't suppose that I could ever expect Dozer to behave like that?" he asked, hoping for the hopeless.

"I don't see why not," Doreen replied, tilting her head to one side as she spoke. "It's going to take work on both your parts, but there is no reason you can't get your dog to behave. Want to start now?"

He looked again at Doreen's dog, who was still sitting by her side, good as gold. Could it really happen to him? "Yes, please," he replied, trying not to look like a kid at Christmas.

Doreen cleared her throat, then frowned. "Just don't expect miracles, Edwin. This is probably the first time you've ever tried anything like this, isn't it?"

"Can you tell?"

She closed her eyes for a second, then sighed loudly. "Okay, let's go out to the open area behind the house." Doreen turned to Gretchen and made a swooping motion with her hand, moving her palm downward, and then changed it to a pushing motion in midair. Gretchen lay down on her haunches, not moving, except for the lolling motion of her tongue as she panted. Doreen pointed the way, and led Edwin and Dozer behind the house.

With a note of satisfaction, Edwin noticed that Gretchen was nowhere in sight. "Where's your dog?" he asked, inwardly gloating, as they rounded the corner to arrive behind the house. So much for her well-trained, perfect schnauzer. He straightened his back.

"I told her to lie down and stay. She'll come when she's called."

"You did? I didn't hear you." No words had been spoken, she had only waved at the dog with some odd sort of hand motions.

"I did it with hand signals. But since she can't see around the corner, I will have to call her." Doreen turned so as not to yell in Edwin's ear. "Gretchen, come," she called out firmly, once. No pleading, no begging, no repeating herself. Doreen was silent.

Within seconds, the dog appeared at a run around the corner, then faithfully sat in front of Doreen, who rewarded her with a gentle pat on the head.

"Wow," was Edwin's only response, accompanied by a dirty look toward his own mutt, who was pulling at the leash for all he was worth to get at Gretchen.

"Come on, I'll show you how it's done, but you have to practice every day. We start with basic 'sit' and 'heel' and 'come,' and then we'll move on to the rest another day."

Patiently, Doreen showed Edwin how to make his dog behave, walking and helping him through the lessons, telling him that there was no such thing as a bad dog, just bad dog owners, with the exception of certain breeds. Within a short hour, he felt he had made progress, and promised to practice every day.

"So when will you take him during the day?" He hoped for Monday, because they had made so much progress in one short lesson.

"When he will come on command the first time I call him, however long it takes," she replied. "Your score slowly has been catching up to Dozer's, but unfortunately, Edwin, the dog's score remains in the lead."

He had no idea what she meant, and he didn't dare to ask. It sounded like a polite way of saying maybe in a million years they'd be ready, so he steeled his nerve, and tried a different approach. "Have you thought about going out with me again? Wanna take in a movie? Or go out for dinner again? If you're pressed for time, we can just have a quick coffee and dessert. I'll even promise to do everything you say with the dog."

Doreen tried not to groan. The obedience lessons were for his benefit, not hers. She stared into his face, trying to decide what to say. Despite his good-natured protests, she thought she'd made it perfectly clear she had no intention of going out with him again; yet he apparently didn't give up. He'd already resorted to begging the other day, and she'd caved in. She wouldn't put it past him to drop to his knees and make a scene, which wouldn't have made any difference, since they were at her house, and alone.

Edwin arched an eyebrow and winked. Doreen melted. "You win. I wouldn't mind a coffee, but I can always put on a pot here rather than going out."

Edwin didn't want to be her guest in her home. He wanted to take her out, charm her, to play the gallant male. He wanted to impress her. But, on the other hand, an invitation from Doreen into her home was progress. He'd take it.

The role reversal intrigued him. Unlike most of the

women he went out with, Doreen was not actively man-hunting, with him being the object of the chase. In fact, just the opposite. He knew she was trying to tell him nicely that she wasn't interested, but yet, if he continued on his light-hearted casual pursuit, maybe some day she would feel the same way about him that he felt about her. Not that he believed in love at first sight, he wasn't that foolish. But the pull on his heartstrings was like nothing he'd ever experienced before, and he couldn't stop thinking about her.

He stepped forward, bringing them within touching distance. With a lump in his throat and his heart on his sleeve, he reached out and touched her hand, then gently massaged her wrist with his thumb. "If all you want is coffee, that's fine, but I'd prefer to take you out, Doreen," he said demurely, gazing into her eyes. He gave her a lopsided smile, then gave her hand a gentle squeeze. "How about lunch? There's a great deli not far from my place, and that will give me a chance to take Dozer home." Smiling his best lady-killer smile, he awaited her answer.

Doreen stared at him, her mouth gaping, then yanked her hand back. His smile heightened his dimples, and the most attractive little crinkles appeared in the corners of his deep brown eyes. The man could be in commercials. "Quit trying to charm me, Edwin. I'm wise to you."

He didn't even have the grace to look contrite. All he did was widen the smile. Trouble was, even though she knew what he was doing, she was falling for it. She rubbed her wrist, then backed up a step. "Give me a minute to lock up, and I'll be right back."

Turning to Gretchen, she made another hand signal, ending with pointing to the house, and Gretchen galloped to the front door and hopped through a doggie door. "I made that one up. I told her to get back in the house. I hope you're taking notes."

"Of course. Do you doubt me?"

Doreen mumbled to herself rather than comment. She utilized the time she used to go inside and fetch her keys to organize her thoughts. The man was going to drive her crazy. Lost in thought after she locked the front door, she automatically stepped toward her van.

She heard the sound of Edwin clearing his throat. "I thought we'd take my car, that is, if you don't have any objections. You don't want to bruise my fragile male ego, do you?" He placed one hand over his heart, making a great show of acting wounded.

Doreen doubted his ego was the least bit fragile. The thought had crossed her mind to take her own vehicle so he wouldn't have to drive her home, but he was laying it on a little thick.

In fact, he played downright dirty. When she opened her mouth to politely object, he smiled impishly, showing off his dimples and a beautiful set of sparkling white teeth to their best advantage. Doreen suspected that he knew exactly how good-looking he was, and used it to his advantage.

Doreen bowed her head and covered her face with her hands. She did object to going in his car with him. She didn't want to get personally involved with Edwin. He was a prospective client, not a date, and she was determined to remain professional. Other clients needed dog obedience lessons. What made him different?

By the time she opened her eyes, Edwin was standing beside his car, holding the passenger door open for her. When he knew he had her attention, he bowed and swept his arm in the direction of the seat, inviting her in.

She couldn't help but smile. Never before had any man

been so persistent, or tried so hard. It was a treat to be catered to, and flattering to be courted, and she knew she was being courted. As sheltered a life as she had led, she had no doubt of his intentions. She resolved not to fall for them.

"What about all the extra mileage you'll be putting on?"

Again, he flashed her a perfect smile. "Your van is worse on gas than my car. And I don't mind driving you back home. In fact, I insist."

As he held out his hand once more, all her resolve melted. Mr. Right, he was not, but he was nice, and, judging from past experience, she knew she would have a pleasant afternoon with him.

"All right, we'll take your car," she sighed. Her voice lowered to a mumble. "How do I get myself into these things?"

"Did you say something?"

Fortunately, he closed the door for her, then jogged around to his side, sparing the need to reply. Dozer already waited in the back seat, for once sitting still.

The conversation on the drive to his house remained light, allowing Doreen to relax and enjoy herself. Once they arrived at Edwin's house, it took only a few minutes to put Dozer inside so they could continue on their way.

The deli turned out to be a small, comfortable family-owned eatery, and judging by Edwin's familiarity with the staff and some of the other customers, he was no stranger here. A robust, gray-haired lady showed them to a small table, and laughed as she asked if they wanted menus. Edwin laughed back, indicating some sort of private joke.

"I don't see anything funny about the menu," Doreen teased, turning and examining it dramatically, as if studying it intently.

Realizing she was pulling his leg, Edwin gave her that impish grin that she was starting to know and love. "I come here all the time, and she knows I have it memorized." His menu remained unopened on the table. "She knows what I want. Care for a demonstration?"

The way he asked almost seemed like a dare. After making her choice, Doreen closed her menu and laid it on the table. "You're on."

The gray-haired lady returned. "You folks decided?"

Edwin winked at the lady, and she responded with a playful snort and tapped her pencil on her order pad. "I'm entertaining a lady friend, I'm happy, and I'm hungry. What do I want today, Marge?"

Marge scribbled on the small pad and tucked his menu into her apron pocket. "And what'll you have, Miss?" she asked, pencil poised.

Doreen raised her eyebrows at the most unusual method of ordering she had ever seen. "Are you two related?"

The older lady laughed heartily. "Only by frequency and familiarity."

Doreen made her selection, Marge scribbled down her order, and was off with a friendly wave of her chubby hand.

"Just how often do you come here?"

Edwin grinned impishly. "Often."

"So, what did you order?"

He tapped his chin with his index finger and closed one eye as he appeared to be running through a mental list of possibilities. "Now if I were to follow Marge's way of reasoning, I said I was entertaining a lady friend, that's you," he paused long enough to make her blush, "so my guess is that it'll be something without ketchup or sauce to dribble down the front of me when I'm eating. No offensive onions or garlic." One hand fanned in front of his mouth as he grinned. "I'm happy, so it doesn't have to be my current favorite, it might even be good for me. Also, I'm hungry, so I know she's going to give me the larger size. Bet she brings me a shrimp sandwich. And no fries, something else. But not a green salad, because salads are for girls, so betcha she brings potato salad."

Edwin rested his elbows on the table, then folded his hands in front of him. "There. That's what I'm having for lunch."

Sure enough, when their lunch arrived, Marge placed a shrimp sandwich with potato salad in front of him.

He was not too ashamed to gloat. Doreen wondered if he was ever serious about anything. She paused for a moment to see if he would pray before their meal. When instead he took a huge bite from his sandwich, she quietly said grace to herself and began to eat. It was just another indication that his priorities were different from hers.

She was partway into her first bite when Edwin spoke. "Nice place you have out there in the middle of nowhere. How long have you lived out there?"

Waving her hand while she chewed, she wondered if his timing was deliberate. Unable to speak with a mouthful, Doreen shrugged her shoulders. He waited politely while she gulped it down. "About two years, but I spent many summers there as a child. It was my Uncle Doug's property, and he willed it to me when he died. If it wasn't for that, I would never have been able to afford to start up my business. I only need a few more dogs, and I'll be making a decent living."

"I guess it keeps you busy."

She shrugged her shoulders. "Not really. I start around ten, the dogs run free for most of the afternoon, and I'm always home by supper time."

"Really? Well, are you busy Thursday after work? Want to go to a barbecue?"

"Depends what time. I've got practice at seven."

"Practice? What are you practicing?"

"For Sunday morning church service. The worship team gets together every Thursday to practice."

"Oh. The barbecue starts at six-thirty, after everyone is home from work. The whole neighborhood is invited, and everybody's encouraged to bring a guest."

"Sorry. It probably would have been fun, but you'll have to find yourself another guest."

Just the thought of bringing someone else took all the appeal out of going. "Well, if the barbecue is out, how would you like to get together another day so you can check up on how I'm doing on my obedience training?"

"I think next Saturday would be soon enough. That gives you a week to practice."

"But that's a week away!" He was hoping to see her again sooner than that.

She shrugged her shoulders, then dabbed her lips with her napkin. "Sorry, but I'm busy all week."

"I guess next Saturday will have to do," he grumbled.

Doreen tilted her head as she tried to analyze what was going on in his head, but dismissed it. *I probably don't want to know.*

Even though he knew she was trying to keep her distance, Edwin refused to give up. He knew she liked him, deep down; otherwise, she would simply tell him to get lost. The fact that she hadn't greatly encouraged him had not deterred him. Every time they got together, he enjoyed himself more, and even though she wouldn't admit it, he knew she did too. He wished he could figure out her hesitation to begin dating him on a regular basis. He had to see her more than once a week. He simply had to figure out how.

When Edwin dropped Doreen off, Gretchen sat beside the front door, wagging her stumpy tail, patiently waiting for Doreen to call her before she came running to greet them. Before Doreen unlocked the house, she hugged Gretchen, then ran her hand down the dog's back. Turning, she waved good-bye to Edwin, then stepped inside and closed the door behind her.

Edwin waved back as she disappeared. If he had a tail, he was sure it would be wagging when Doreen greeted him, too.

He was going to have to come up with some reason to see her before next Saturday, but what?

six

Edwin checked his tie in the rearview mirror. It was as straight as he knew it would be, no different from when he checked it at the last red light. Likewise, his hair was perfect, not a single strand out of place.

He drew a deep breath to steel himself. It wasn't like he had never been to church before. In fact, he'd just been to church last. . .when was that now? Mother's Day last year? Okay, so it had been a while. Who was counting? He'd been dragged off to church millions of times as a little kid. He didn't have to be nervous. He knew all about God and stuff.

As he walked through the parking lot toward the main door among the other churchgoers, he tried to take note nonchalantly of how everyone else was dressed. This morning he had struggled with what to wear, and had gone the middle route, choosing his best black slacks, a sedate-colored shirt, and a black tie, and judging from everyone around him as they filed into the building, he had made a good choice. Some men were wearing suits, and there were some young men wearing jeans. No one seemed uncomfortable, so he decided he didn't either. And he hoped God wouldn't strike him down for lying to himself.

At the door, an older man in a suit stopped Edwin to shake his hand and exchange a few words of welcome as he presented Edwin with a bulletin and a few other assorted papers. Edwin had no desire to stop and chat. Strains of music softly echoed from the sanctuary, drawing him like a magnet.

He had expected somber organ music and old-fashioned hymns, but the music he heard as he stepped into the sanctuary could have been a selection from an easy-listening station. Up at the front, on a slightly elevated platform stage, a young man with his hair tied back in a ponytail strummed a bright-red electric guitar. Behind him was a casually dressed man playing the drums. A balding man in a suit and tie was plunking a bass guitar, and behind a large, glossy black grand piano sat Doreen. Together, they played beautiful music.

Edwin was intrigued by the contemporary decor of the sanctuary. The place was crowded with people either standing in the aisles or sitting in the rows of padded chairs. People mingled everywhere, happily chatting in small groups.

Edwin picked an empty seat in the aisle nearest the piano, and sat back to listen. This was church music? Now he knew why Doreen needed to practice every week. There was more to this music than simply following the notes in a songbook.

At the stroke of ten, a man stepped up to a microphone at the front, welcomed everyone, and encouraged those still standing to find a seat. As soon as everyone was sitting, however, he asked the congregation to stand. The band started on cue with a loud, rousing praise song; everyone joined in, most of them clapping their hands. The words were projected onto a screen suspended from the ceiling.

Edwin tried to follow along, but mostly he was moved by the evident energy in the crowd. This was like nothing he had ever experienced before. The words were inspiring, the music was uplifting, and the atmosphere in the church was joyful, as everyone praised God in unison.

After a number of upbeat selections, the music quieted to a background level, and the worship leader instructed the congregation to bow their heads while he led a short prayer.

Closing his eyes, Edwin said a prayer of his own, asking God what was going on, and why he was trembling. When the leader had finished his prayer, he told everyone to greet those around them. The music continued to play gently in the background. Doreen sat with her eyes still closed and her head bobbed rhythmically as she played the piano.

Edwin didn't know what to do. He didn't know a soul around him, and he suddenly felt shy, which was unusual for him. When a hand lightly touched his shoulder, he tried not to flinch. He turned to see a nicely dressed couple about his age smiling at him from the row behind him.

"Hi," the man said, extending his hand. "I'm Richard, and this is my wife Evelyn."

Edwin accepted Richard's handshake and smiled nervously. "Hi, my name is Edwin."

"First time here?" Richard asked. Evelyn smiled warmly at him.

Edwin nodded. He wondered exactly how out of place he looked, and how many could tell he didn't belong here.

"Thought so, you looked nervous." Richard's smile widened. "Don't be. Everyone is very friendly and open here, and at one time or another we've all felt what you're feeling. But we want you to feel welcome."

Edwin couldn't think of a thing to say. This was certainly different from his mother's old-fashioned church.

"Care to join us for lunch later? A lot of us meet at the local pancake house for brunch after the service, and you're welcome to come and meet everyone."

"Uh, actually I'm here with the piano player, she just

doesn't know it yet." Edwin's eyes wandered over to Doreen, who diligently worked the keyboard.

Richard and Evelyn's eyes met for a brief second, glanced toward Doreen, then back to Edwin. Evelyn chuckled. "Doreen McCullough? Oh, we know Doreen. She doesn't know you're here?"

Edwin grinned. He didn't even know he was coming until this morning. He wondered what Doreen's reaction would be when she finally saw him. "No. It's a surprise."

The music rose in volume, and the man at the front led another rousing chorus, causing the whole building to ring out in song.

Edwin satisfied himself with reading the words as the melody played, contemplating the meaning as each song progressed. By the time the music drew to a finish, he was surprised to discover a lump in his throat. The moving words made him think in ways he never had before, delving deep into his soul to discover he didn't know God as much as he thought he did. It left him feeling strangely empty, and he didn't know what to do about it.

After the music stopped, Edwin continue to stare at the screen, reading the words one more time before the projector shut off. Lost in thought, he almost missed Doreen as the musicians vacated the front platform to allow the pastor to speak. Blinking rapidly a few times to clear his eyes as well as his head, he waved and called out to her in a low voice as she passed.

"Edwin?" she whispered. A look of semi-shock crossed her face, followed by a wide ear-to-ear smile. "Hi!" she whispered as she slid in beside him. "Good to see you here! I've been thinking about you, and now I know why."

As the pastor started his message, Edwin sat in stunned silence. During the short car ride to the church, he had envisioned plans to hold Doreen's hand and whisper play-ful secrets to her during the service. Instead, he found his attention glued to the words of the sermon as he sat somberly, listening with undivided attention.

The words gripped him. The pastor's topic was commit-ments. Commitment to your friends, commitment to your loved ones, commitment to yourself and your goals, com-mitment to God, and above all, God's commitment to His children. The pastor pointed around the congregation to emphasize his point, and at one point appeared to be point-ing right at Edwin. He shrank back in his seat.

When the sermon was done, the pastor called to the front anyone who wanted to commit their lives to Christ, or anyone who wanted prayer. Edwin struggled with con-flicting impulses, but he stayed glued to his chair. He wished he could grab Doreen's hand, which had been His plan all along, but she had gone back to the platform to play the piano while the pastor offered the invitation.

Everyone bowed their heads as the pastor closed the ser-vice in prayer. Edwin stared at the floor and tried to sort out his thoughts. When the time came to leave, he remained seated.

When Doreen finally made her way back to him, he said, "I went to church all the time as a kid, Doreen. Why is this so different?"

Doreen placed her hand lightly on his shoulder and squeezed. As far as Edwin was concerned she might as well have been squeezing his heart. He clenched his teeth. She patted his shoulder softly as she spoke. "Because today it's personal, Edwin. Today it's just between you and God."

A million thoughts zinged through his head, trying to connect everything that had happened to him in the past hour and a half. Rather than look like an idiot sitting there as everyone else filed out, Edwin rose to his feet and left the sanctuary with Doreen.

"Every Sunday after the service, a bunch of us go out for lunch to the local pancake restaurant. Do you want to go so I can introduce you around, or should we go somewhere else?"

To her own surprise, Doreen actually anticipated the opportunity to introduce Edwin to her friends. She held her breath, awaiting his reply.

The color returned to his face and he nodded, smiling more like the Edwin she was getting to know. "Sure, let's join them. I met a real nice couple at the start of the service, and they mentioned the same thing. Richard and Evelyn. I guess you know them."

"Oh? You met Richard and Evelyn? They're really nice. She's pregnant."

Edwin's eyes twinkled and one eyebrow quirked. Doreen gasped and covered her mouth with both hands. Whatever possessed her to say such a thing? And to him, of all people.

"They look like they'll make good parents." He looked around at the nearly empty lot. "What do you want to do, take one vehicle or two? How crowded does this restaurant get?"

"Pretty crowded. It probably would be easier to take one car. If you don't mind you can drop me off back here later, although sometimes I just like to kill time. I've got to be back at six for the evening service."

"You can come to my place, then, while you wait." In the absence of a reply, he continued. "Now let's join your friends for lunch. Point the way."

❧

Name tags definitely would have been an asset. It seemed

Doreen's church friends had a whole section of the restaurant reserved on an ongoing basis. Doreen introduced him to so many people that the only ones he could remember were Bill, the owner of the pet store, his wife Edna, the couple he had already met, and a few select others. The crowd ranged from a lady who was ninety-five if she was a day, to a small baby who was, thankfully, fast asleep.

He almost regretted when it was time to leave, but even though he thoroughly enjoyed visiting, he decided to be selfish and take Doreen home to have her all to himself.

When he drove past the church on the way to his house, Doreen opened her mouth as if to protest, but he shook his head and winked, and didn't stop talking. She sighed and shrugged her shoulders once, but didn't interrupt the conversation or change the subject. Edwin considered that a point in his favor.

_≈

After they reached Edwin's house and had survived Dozer's usual front door ruckus, Doreen settled onto the living room couch while Edwin sorted through his CD collection for something appropriate.

He could tell by her expression that she wanted to ask him something, but if it was a question about why he had gone to church, he wasn't prepared to answer. To be honest, he had only gone to try to startle and impress Doreen. The uplifting time of singing and the pastor's sermon had completely rearranged his perspective. He still had to sort it out in his own mind before he would be ready to talk about it. He'd never thought about being selected personally by God himself, or that God would care on a daily basis what he said and did.

His thoughts were interrupted by the sound of a car alarm screaming in the street. Dozer went berserk. Bounding over the ottoman, he raced toward the front door. When his paws touched the linoleum floor, he proceeded to slide, all four legs clambering for some form of traction, and failing that, he landed with a crash against the door. He jumped up and down and barked wildly until the alarm was silenced. When satisfied that whatever was out there was gone, he slowly returned to the living room to sit in front of Edwin.

"Stupid dog." His fingers rounded the dog's snout and gave it a playful squeeze. "So you're going to church again tonight?" he asked Doreen, leaning back as he sank into the soft couch. With a thump he rested his feet on the coffee table and pulled his tie loose, letting it hang in a wide circle around his neck. "You play three times every Sunday?"

Casually, Dozer jumped on the couch to lay down beside Edwin, and Edwin absently reached over to scratch him. Dozer's eyes closed, and the dog started to drift off to sleep beneath his master's touch.

Doreen watched the lazy scene before her. This was the same dog that only minutes ago had crashed into the front door? Edwin not only allowed, but encouraged his dog to jump up on the furniture? She knew from the telltale dog hair at her own house that Gretchen made a habit of sitting on the couch, but only when Doreen wasn't around to watch.

"Yes, I play for all three services every Sunday. At the moment, we don't have another piano player." Doreen thought back to her first sight of Edwin at church, and compared him to the carefree man before her now, idly scratching his dog.

Up until today, she couldn't take Edwin seriously, but this morning another side of him became visible. She had half expected him to fool around during the service, making jokes and talking, but he had surprised her. Not only did he sit still, but he had paid rapt attention, listening intently to every word that was said. Even though he hadn't talked about it, she knew something had changed, and she hoped it was God moving in his heart. Through experience, and despite her curiosity, she forced herself to wait until he was ready to talk about it. She only hoped she would be able to answer any questions he would have, when and if they came. She didn't remember exactly when she had started praying for him, but now she determined that her prayers would be more diligent.

The dog started to snore. Edwin kept scratching him. "So what does Gretchen do while you're gone all day? That must mean that you leave at what, eight-thirty in the morning, and you don't get back until nine at night? That's a long lonely day for a dog."

Doreen shrugged her shoulders. "I'm sure she misses me, but she has her doggie door, and she keeps busy chasing birds and squirrels on my property."

Edwin smiled as he examined his spoiled, sleeping city dog, continuing to pat him. "I guess your neighbors are far enough away, then."

Doreen didn't understand what he meant. "Far away? From what?" she asked.

"The noise," he replied. "Oh, let me guess," the tone of his voice changed to include a hint of disgust. "Your perfect dog never barks or howls."

"Of course my dog barks. All dogs bark, just some more than others. But she certainly doesn't howl." Her gaze drifted from Edwin to Dozer. "Let me guess. From the sound of your statement, Dozer howls."

"I was told it was common for schnauzers to howl. Mine does. I'm sure yours does too."

"She most certainly does not."

"You don't know that for sure. If it weren't for my neighbor, I would never have known."

"I beg your pardon?"

"My neighbor from across the street told me that sometimes Dozer howls for hours. I didn't believe her, so one day I left and parked the car a few blocks away and walked back. I thought I heard something, but he stopped when he heard me coming."

"He howls for hours?"

He stopped touching Dozer, leaned back into the couch, and crossed his arms over his chest. "Maybe Gretchen howls, but you've never heard her. Dozer only howls when I leave. Old Mrs. Primline is convinced that he's in terrible pain, but I asked the vet, and he said it's quite common for schnauzers to howl. My neighbor seems more worried than annoyed, which is a good thing, because there's nothing I can do about it."

Dozer snorted in his sleep, then slowly rolled onto his back with all four legs sticking in the air. When Edwin began to rub his stomach, Dozer's head lolled to the side, tilting over the edge of the couch. Edwin appeared unconcerned.

He stood, leaving his dog upside down on the couch. "If we have to be back at the church soon, we should probably think about what we're going to do for supper."

Doreen closed one eye as she watched him disappear around the corner into the kitchen. We? Admittedly she was at his mercy for transportation, having left her van in the parking lot at the church, but she had not considered a dinner invitation to be forthcoming.

The refrigerator door closed, and Edwin returned. "After that huge late lunch, I'm not hungry, but we'll probably be starving right in the middle of the thing tonight. I can make us a sandwich or fry up a couple eggs if you want.

Unless you want to grab a quick burger on our way."

"You're coming to the evening service?"

"Why not? Am I not invited?"

The question scared Doreen and at the same time excited her. She wasn't naive enough to discard the likelihood that he had attended church this morning just to see her. But if he wanted to attend another service, it was her duty as a Christian to help and encourage him in any way possible in his efforts to seek God. The possibility gave her courage.

"Of course you're invited. I was just surprised that you wanted to go, that's all."

He checked his watch. "I guess we should leave in half an hour. Want something?"

Doreen shook her head, still contemplating his desire to accompany her. "No, nothing for me. I couldn't think of eating another bite."

"Well, if you'll excuse me, I'm going to make something for myself." He disappeared back into the kitchen. Dozer shifted his position in his sleep, with one shoulder in addition to his head hanging further over the edge of the couch.

"Uh, Edwin, is that dog safe? He's making me nervous. He looks like he's going to—"

Dozer's head shifted further over the edge, followed by the other shoulder. He continued to slide until, just as Doreen feared, he fell off the couch and landed with a thump on the floor. Dazed, he stood, wobbled for a step, then slowly plodded to a blanket in the corner of the room, where he lay down and fell back to sleep immediately.

Doreen couldn't believe her eyes. "That dog's not normal."

Edwin returned from the kitchen, munching on a sandwich. "Naw. He's just a little clumsy."

The dog was clumsy, undisciplined, untrained, and howled like a banshee. And she considered taking him as a client? Was she crazy? One look at Edwin, leaning on one hip in the doorway holding a plate in one hand and eating with the other, made her realize that she had gotten herself in too deep with Edwin to turn back now. She could always pray for a miracle.

Edwin pushed the last bite of the sandwich into his mouth with two fingers, and turned back into the kitchen, leaving her alone in the living room with the snoring dog.

seven

The answering machine light flashed insistently as Doreen walked in after dropping off the last of the dogs. Anxiously, she pressed the button and waited to hear the three messages, hoping at least one of them was a new customer.

The first was a wrong number.

The second was Edwin, calling to say hello on his lunch break.

The third was Edwin, calling to say hello on his coffee break.

The tape had not finished rewinding when the phone rang.

"Walking The Dog," Doreen answered.

"Hi Doreen! It's Edwin!"

Doreen covered her face with one hand. "I should have guessed."

"What? Why?"

"I just finished listening to your voice on the answering machine, and I'm not even finished rewinding the tape, and here you are again. What can I do for you?"

"I think I've got Dozer ready. When do you want to take him?"

After the performances his dog had made recently, Doreen had good reason to disbelieve Edwin's bold claim. Only four days since their lesson, she highly doubted that Dozer was a dog prodigy. "I don't think four days is long enough to adequately train a dog. Even one as bright as Dozer."

"Ah!" he exclaimed enthusiastically, "but you should see how he's improved. You wouldn't think it's the same dog! Really!"

She really doubted it. "Why don't you give it a little more time, and I'll see for myself on Saturday."

"Aw, come on, Doreen," he begged. "Please?"

Doreen squeezed her eyes shut, pinched the bridge of her nose, shook her head, and sighed. "All right, bring him over."

"Great! See you soon. And don't eat supper." He hung up without waiting for her response.

What had she done?

❧

Gretchen barked and ran to the door, signifying Edwin's arrival. "Stay." Doreen gave the hand signal to stay and opened the door.

A scene very different than the last time awaited her as she stood in her open doorway, waiting, watching Edwin and Dozer in action.

To her surprise, Dozer sat motionless in the front passenger seat, perfectly behaved as Edwin leaned into the back seat, groping for something. Edwin sat upright, honked Dozer's long snout with his free hand, and exited the car carrying a large pizza box. He slammed the door shut and walked up to her without his dog.

"Watch this." He handed her the pizza and turned to the car. He cleared his throat for effect. "Dozer, come," he commanded sternly.

Obediently, Dozer lunged out the open car window, landed with his feet scrambling, scattering gravel in all directions, and bounded to Edwin, jumping up on him for recognition of his good behavior.

"Wasn't that great!" Edwin exclaimed proudly as Dozer

continued to jump up and down. After a few futile swipes attempting to remove the paw prints from his shirt, he gave up. "He's a little excited right now, but didn't he do good?" Edwin's eyes shone, as proud of himself as he was of his dog.

Doreen tried to evaluate them objectively. While not the most dignified performance, the dog had stayed sitting when commanded, and he had come when called. "It's an improvement, but I'm not sure it's good enough to take him. First, he must obey and come for me."

Edwin beamed ear to ear. "First, can we eat this pizza before it gets cold?"

With a shrug of her shoulders, Doreen headed into the house, hoping the supper break would give her time to think. Edwin followed on her heels with Gretchen following behind Edwin. Dozer sneaked to the front, directly underneath the pizza box, eyeing it with every step she took.

"Are we going to have another lesson on Saturday? We've been working really hard, and I think we're ready for the next step."

"Well, we'll have to work more on 'come.'" She hated to disappoint him and tell him that a proper "come" meant for the dog to sit in front of his master quietly when called, awaiting the next command without movement. "We'll start on 'heel,' too. By the way, the proper signal for stay is to show your palm to the dog's face, not grab the poor thing's nose."

"But it's such a big nose," he snickered, closing the door behind him.

Because Dozer was starting to act too territorial around the pizza box, Doreen shooed both dogs outside and locked the doggie door shut. They ran into the yard, taking turns chasing each other, and Edwin opened the pizza.

"What are you doing here at this hour?" Doreen asked, turning her back to him as she selected two plates from the cupboard. "I thought you didn't get home until much later."

Edwin scooped out two pieces of the most well-loaded pizza Doreen had ever seen, laying them gently on the plates without a single mushroom falling off. "They owed me some time, so I left early. I wanted to see you this evening."

She didn't want to know why, but suspected obedience lessons for the dog was merely an excuse. "So," she licked her fingers between bites, "you've been practicing."

"Mmm," he mumbled, swallowing his last bite before helping himself to another piece. "I wanted you to take him as soon as possible. I've had to work a lot of overtime lately, and the traffic is getting so much worse. It's getting too long to have him locked inside. I wonder whether that's why he's howling so much."

"I doubt it. Unfortunately, the breed is prone to howling."

"My friend's kid says it's because he's sad. My neighbor says it's his teeth."

"His teeth?" The dog didn't look old enough to require dental care.

"My neighbor is constantly complaining about her dentures, so she's completely convinced that Dozer howls because he has a toothache."

Doreen packed up the pizza box and set the glasses in the dishwasher. A toothache? Doreen couldn't help but wonder about this neighbor.

Looking toward the door, Doreen wondered where the dogs were, since neither of them had been around to beg for pizza. Then she remembered that she had locked them out.

"If Dozer responds as well as you're leading me to believe, I can hardly wait to see for myself."

Even outside behind the house, the dogs were nowhere to be seen. "He'll come. You'll see. I'll call him, and then you can start looking after him." Edwin inhaled deeply and opened his mouth to call Dozer, but Doreen stopped him. She had a plan.

"I'll make a deal with you. This is the kind of situation where I'll need him to come to me when I call, when he's off playing with the other dogs. If he comes for me now, I'll take him tomorrow. If not, you have to work with him some more."

"Deal." He offered her his hand to shake on it, but when she slid her hand into his, he covered both of their hands, then started to trail his fingertips delicately and teasingly up her arm. His smile reeked of an invitation Doreen wanted no part of. She yanked her hand back, and tried to ignore him, despite her wobbly knees.

"Here goes." Doreen sucked in a deep breath. "Dozer, come!" she called. Once. She knew he wouldn't come, it was part of her plan.

They waited. And waited. Doreen had turned with a smirk to tell him his dog wasn't coming when she heard snapping underbrush and rustling branches in the distance. With one final crunch, Dozer loped into the clearing, heading straight for Doreen.

"Well, I'll be. . ." She had been so confident he wouldn't come. Now she would have to eat crow and do as she had promised. Unable to stop staring as Dozer approached, she had no alternative but to take him as a client, even though he wasn't really ready. She would take him, but she smelled trouble.

Many times over the past few days, she had caught herself

thinking of Edwin, and along with visions of his smiling eyes, she remembered his reaction to the Sunday morning message. If he was starting to see God in a different light as an adult, she could do nothing to encumber his discovery process.

"Where's your dog? See, mine came, and yours didn't," he taunted. Edwin couldn't help but gloat. Even though she never said it out loud, she left the impression that she compared her perfect Gretchen to poor old Dozer, and Dozer always came up short. This time, he had her.

"I didn't call Gretchen. I only called Dozer." She pulled a dog whistle out of her pocket and blew it. Sure enough, Gretchen came running.

"You were saying?"

"Hmmph," he mumbled. "Nothing."

"What are you grousing about? You won fair and square. I'll take Dozer starting tomorrow. Would you like to discuss terms and conditions?"

"Terms?"

"Terms for payment, and we'll draw up a contract for times, days, plus special requirements, such as medication."

He didn't feel right discussing money with her. Despite the fact that she was providing a service he obviously needed, it cheapened the relationship.

"I take cash, checks, or credit card debits."

His heart caught in his throat. Relationship? As much as he would have liked to call it that, they didn't have anything close to being called a relationship.

When they first met, he only looked at her business card for her phone number to ask her out, but after he thought about it, he knew he should use her services. He was already guilt-ridden about leaving poor Dozer alone for such a long time, and Doreen provided him with an opportunity to do something about it. But now, to be discussing business and money didn't sit well with him. He wanted to move on to the relationship part. Instead, he followed her back inside the house, into a room that had been converted to an office, to complete the paperwork.

The office suited the rest of the small house. Earlier, it had taken all the finesse he could muster not to comment on the spotless little dwelling. She had converted the small, two-bedroom cottage into a very comfortable living space. Every inch in the kitchen was used to its full potential; likewise the living room. Her tasteful furniture matched the mood of the house, containing everything she needed without being crowded.

Her tiny office barely held a desk complete with a computer, a filing cabinet, and two chairs for visitors. Like the rest of the house, it too was immaculate. Baskets contained any loose pieces of paper, a compact organizer held pens, paper clips, and other office necessities. A framed photograph of Gretchen with a white prize ribbon tacked to it graced the wall directly across from the desk.

Edwin watched as she retrieved her blank forms. When she bent over and leaned way to the back of the filing cabinet drawer, he turned to look out the window to distract himself. *What am I thinking? This woman is a devout churchgoer.* He wanted to keep everything on the up-and-up.

"Here Edwin, all you need to do is read it and sign on the dotted line. I filled in the times I'll be picking Dozer up and dropping him off. Just make sure you agree, and we're done."

At the sight of her innocent smile, his heart pounded in his chest. Holding out the pen for him, she raised her head and pushed the paper across the desk.

He signed the waiver without reading it, and he quickly scanned the other document, making a mental note of the times she would be by, then pushed it back.

Doreen stood, peeled a carbonless copy off the back and handed it to him. She placed the top copy in the basket in the corner of her desk, then stood. "There we go. It's a done deal." She smiled sweetly into his face with those big blue eyes that almost made his knees give out, and held out her hand to shake on it.

He glanced down at her delicate hand, then at the desk separating them. He had never wanted to kiss a woman so badly. He sidestepped the desk and stood beside her. Her eyes opened even wider as she stared up at him. He didn't know what to do.

Should he reach out and pull her in and hold her the way he wanted? Should he give her a little peck on the cheek? Should he kiss her on the mouth? Should he slowly and seductively give her a long and heated kiss she'd never forget? He wouldn't forget, that was for sure. Would he put his arms around her and press her body up to his or seductively cup her face? All he knew was that he was as nervous as a sixteen-year-old out on his first date.

Doreen cleared her throat, breaking the spell. He settled for shaking her hand without trying anything funny. The last time he tried something, she had yanked her hand away so fast he might have been on fire. He pulled at the collar on his shirt. Speaking of fire, it was a little warm in the small room.

"Did you bring a key?"

"Key?"

"I'll need your house key to get Dozer while you're at work."

"Oh, I never thought of that. I'll have to make one for

you. I guess this means you can't pick him up tomorrow."

"Looks that way."

Edwin grinned, then tried not to laugh at her confused expression, no doubt trying to figure out why he was smiling. She'd fallen into his trap by giving him an excuse to come back tomorrow. All the comp time his employer owed him was going to come in handy.

Edwin headed to the door, Dozer faithfully following behind him. "I'll be back tomorrow, same time, with the key. Unless you're busy, that is."

"Actually, I am busy. Sorry."

His heart sank. "Oh."

"It's practice night at church, but I can drop by your place after and pick up the key, if it's not too late."

His mood brightened. It would never be too late. "Go ahead and stop by, whenever. I'll look forward to seeing you."

Doreen watched the dust cloud rise in the air then dissipate as Edwin drove away. He wasn't her type, but yet she couldn't help but like him. He was kind of cute in an endearing sort of way. And she could have sworn that he was going to kiss her. Even though she didn't think a relationship with him would be advisable, she wondered why he hadn't at least tried to kiss her. And why was she disappointed?

❧

Another Thursday, another practice. For the first time, Doreen's heart was not in it. For all the uplifting music, and as much as she felt the communion with God as she played, this time it seemed all her attention focused on the clock.

When practice finally ended, she was the first one out the door. She didn't stay the extra half hour for coffee and chitchat. In her haste to make it out the door, she headed straight into the parking lot rather than to the office to phone Edwin to let him know she was on her way. Besides, she didn't want to hear that he hadn't had time to have a duplicate key made, and cancel her visit.

She remembered surprising him by being early when he asked her out for dinner. Even though she was alone in the car, the thought of Edwin answering the door with his shirt undone and his tie hanging loose made her smile. This time, she didn't expect any such sights to await her, but she anticipated seeing him regardless.

Wild barking announced her arrival as soon as her feet touched the concrete of his driveway. She had barely closed the van door when she heard the dull thud of Dozer hitting the door. Seconds later, Edwin stood in the open doorway, grinning from ear to ear.

"Here I am," said Doreen. "Did you get a key made for me? Sorry I didn't phone before I left. I hope I'm not interrupting anything." She held out her hand and looked at him expectantly.

"Oops, I forgot it upstairs on the table. Would you like to come in?" He gave her an exaggerated wink. "I bought donuts."

"Only if it includes coffee." Her response brought a hearty laugh from Edwin. Not above accepting a bribe, she followed him up the stairs and into the kitchen, where the box of donuts sat on the counter next to the coffeemaker, which was ready and waiting as Edwin flicked the switch. She tried to act surprised.

"Is it decaffeinated?"

He melodramatically covered his heart with one palm. "I'll have you know I made a special trip for the ghastly stuff. I like my coffee loaded and strong, so I hope you appreciate the sacrifice I'm making for you."

"Chalk one up for the gallant knight," she said with a smirk.

The coffeemaker gurgled and hissed as they sat at the table.

"How was practice? I'm looking forward to hearing you play again on Sunday."

"Practice was fine." Practice was lousy, she'd never been so distracted. But rather than dwell on the evening's practice, Doreen concentrated on the other half of his comment. If he was planning to attend church on Sunday, she hoped from the depths of her soul that his only reason was not to see her, but to worship God and hear His word.

"Can I ask you a question?" Edwin shuffled his feet under the table, lowered his head, and stared into his empty cup.

Doreen wasn't sure what to expect, or that she would want to hear what was coming. "I suppose. Go ahead." She clenched her teeth in anticipation.

"What the pastor said on Sunday, about commitment and getting to know God and reading the Bible, do you read the Bible?"

"Yes, I do. Not as often as I intend, but I do." She waited for him to continue, not sure what he was getting at. With Edwin, it could be anything.

"I realized that I don't know as much about God as I thought I did. How do I get to know Him better?"

She settled back in her seat as she recalled the apostle Peter's admonition to be ready to share your faith in or out of season.

"Well, Edwin, you can read the Bible, think about what you read, talk to other believers, and listen to what God has to say to you. Invite Him into your life. He makes His message clear in many forms. Just be open. Does that help?"

"Uh, yeah, it does. Do you have a Bible I can borrow?"

"Borrow? You mean you don't have one?"

"No, I don't. My mother had one, but I couldn't understand the old-style English, so I never bothered."

Wasn't this a goal of every Christian, to give a Bible to a new believer and help lead him to a closer relationship with the Lord? And Edwin, of all people. Doreen tried to keep her heart from fluttering.

"No, I don't have one you can borrow, but I've got one you can have."

"Oh, I couldn't do that. I'll give it back."

"No, really, you can have it. I have more than one."

"No," Edwin shook his head as he spoke. "My mother treasures her old family Bible, I don't want to take something so personal."

Her mind raced to think which translation would be best for him. "Well, I see your point. I'll take it back after you've read the whole thing."

All he did was blink and stare. "Uh, the whole thing?"

"Otherwise, I don't want it back." Doreen was proud of her on-the-spot plan. Either way she won. Or rather, God won. "You have to promise."

"If I didn't know better, I'd think you're taking advantage of my integrity."

"Me?" Doreen copied his earlier gesture, placing her open hand over her heart. "You wound me, sir."

He didn't give her the dignity of a response. He carried on in spite of himself. "I must admit, I'm curious. Okay, I'll try to read the whole thing, if you promise to answer any questions for me."

"I'm looking forward to it." She couldn't think of a better way to spend her time with Edwin. For the little, if anything, they had in common, she enjoyed spending time with him, and now, to share God's word with him would make their friendship so much more special. Even though he got on her nerves at times, Doreen could at least admit she was growing fond of him. She was even starting to get used to his crazy dog.

"Doreen? Are you tired? You seem to be staring into space. Want me to drive you home?" Doreen blinked. Edwin had poured the fragrant, steaming coffee into the mug in front of her, and now stood beside her holding a carton of milk. She had been so lost in thought she hadn't even noticed him get up. The open donut box also sat in front of her, waiting for her to take her pick of all the mouthwatering varieties.

"No, I was just thinking, that's all." She picked the closest donut and bit into it, embarrassed to be caught daydreaming, especially about him, when he was right in front of her.

The conversation changed to less serious matters, and soon Edwin had the two of them laughing and sharing stories as they ate their snack. When she discovered that Edwin had to be up at six in order to be at work by seven-thirty, Doreen excused herself and headed home with his house key.

eight

Doreen pushed the sun visor down to shield her eyes as she turned into Edwin's driveway. Today was her first day on the job with Dozer. She considered herself ten times a fool for doing this. Dozer still required far more intensive personal training, yet here she was, ready to fetch him from the house and load him into a new kennel in the back of her van. She wanted him to behave. She wanted to make a good impression. She wanted to kick herself.

After being locked in the house all day five days a week, all the dogs in her care were ecstatic when allowed to roam free for a couple of hours, and Dozer would likely be no different. However, she remained cautious entering a new client's house the first time to pick up a dog without the owner, and Dozer was no exception. Some dogs could be unpredictable without their owner present.

So far she had never been bitten, but there was always a first time, especially with the protective breeds. It had taken a long time to earn the Doberman's trust, and she had experienced a few close calls with her.

When she had started, the Doberman's owner had made no assurances that the dog would allow her in the house without him present. In order to protect her safety, she had requested an initial trial visit the weekend beforehand, with the owner standing behind her outside as she opened the door.

At the time, the owner frightened Doreen more than the dog. A large, husky biker, complete with tattoos up both arms and a pierced earring in his nose, he had confided in her that the only reason he bought the Doberman was that the day he had the money to buy the dog, he couldn't find a pit bull. In the end, behind the man's rough exterior hid a gruff but gentle man. After all, he had a soft enough heart to hire out her services to see to the dog's needs every day when he wasn't home.

Doreen killed the engine, pausing to make sure the air-conditioning was running for the dog's comfort, and opened the door. Key in hand, she straightened and started the long walk up the sidewalk.

"Are you the dog lady?" a shrill, high-pitched, female voice bellowed from across the street.

Doreen jumped at the grating voice, then cringed. An elderly lady approached, running across the street, waving her hands. This must be the neighbor Edwin had warned her about.

"Yes, I operate the dog care service." Doreen hated being called the dog lady.

The elderly woman faced her squarely, resting one hand on her hip, wagging one finger in the air. "How much do you know about dogs? That animal is in pain, I tell you. That young man won't listen to me, but I hear that animal howling every day, day after day. You know, I think it has a toothache, and I know what I'm talking about."

"Well, I—"

"The poor thing howls every day after Eddie leaves, and I know he means well, but I just don't think that young man realizes how that dog is suffering. I know how the poor thing feels, before I got my dentures I felt like howling too."

Doreen tried to back up a step, to get closer to Edwin's front door. "I'm sure you—"

The neighbor placed her wrinkled hand firmly on Doreen's forearm, preventing her from going any further. The jutting stone from a large, ugly ring dangled from a poor fit, and dug into Doreen's skin. She tried to pull away, but the woman hung on tighter. "And Bulldozer is a good dog, really friendly, and a good watchdog. Why, you should hear how he snarls when the mailman comes every morning. Of course the fact that it's in pain doesn't help. Why, the poor thing even howls after the mailman leaves. The mailman tried pushing dog biscuits through the mail slot for a while. But here's how I know it has a toothache. Bulldozer howls even longer after the mailman leaves now, and he even stopped leaving the dog a biscuit."

Doreen could not keep from smiling. Edwin had told her about the dog's howling, but she had no idea it was this bad. He probably didn't, either. It seemed his neighbor, the self-appointed expert, knew all the answers.

The woman continued. "I wish there was something I could do. After the mailman stopped leaving biscuits, I tried to give him those dog treats they show on TV that clean a dog's teeth, but it didn't do any good. The poor thing howls now when I leave after a visit. I talk to him through the slot when I give him those teeth cleaning biscuits. He's lonely, you know. And poor Eddie is lonely, too. I do my best to visit often to keep him company. He's not going to find a wife with that howling animal. The last woman he saw was—"

Doreen didn't want to hear the sordid details of Edwin's love life. "I know how you can help," Doreen interrupted, attempting to stop the nattering. She knew schnauzers as a breed tended to howl. There was nothing wrong with Edwin's dog that a little training wouldn't cure. Okay, a lot of training.

"Oh? How?" For the first time, the elderly lady remained silent.

"I'm not a veterinarian, but I do know a lot about dogs and their behavior. If you can tell me all about how he howls, then I can tell what's wrong with him." She tried to sound more confident than she felt. The dog howled because it was in his genetic makeup. Labradors like to swim, terriers like to dig, schnauzers like to howl.

The lady cocked her head, stared Doreen in the face for a few seconds, glanced toward Edwin's front door, then back to Doreen. Dozer's echoing barks and thumps drifted through the neighborhood.

"What do you mean, tell you how he howls?" She crossed her arms on her chest and stared Doreen down.

Doreen finally answered only to ease the thick silence. "He isn't howling now, but if you could tell me how he howls, then I might be able to analyze it."

The woman's eyes opened wide. "Really? You can do that?"

Doreen leaned forward as if expressing a secret that no one else was supposed to hear. "But don't tell Edwin what we're doing. You know how he talks to his dog. If he lets the dog catch on, then it won't work."

The neighbor gasped, bringing her gnarled hands to her wrinkled cheeks. "No!" she exclaimed, "You mean you can help them?"

"Yes, but you have to tell me exactly how the dog howls, so I can check up on it."

Looking from side to side to make sure none of the other neighbors were watching, the woman leaned closer, as if caught in an intriguing web.

Doreen whispered. "Study the dog, listen to him, but don't let him catch you. I don't know what it is about dogs, but sometimes if they know they have an audience, they act different." She paused, and the neighbor nodded, sneaking a glance at Edwin's door, as if Dozer were listening. "Can you do it?"

"Yes!" Mrs. Primline exclaimed.

Both of them straightened.

"Then if you'll excuse me, I have to get back to work."

As Doreen started to make her way to Edwin's door once more, the woman called her again.

"Wait!" she called. "I don't know your name."

Turning quickly on her toes, Doreen walked back to her van as fast as she could manage without being obvious she was running. She pulled one of her business cards out of the console, and handed it to the lady.

"My name is Doreen. And please, if you can show me exactly what he sounds like, don't hesitate to call me anytime. This is important." Doreen tried to look serious as she studied the intense concentration on Mrs. Primline's face.

"I'll call you as soon as I can," she rasped as she nodded, then turned to walk back across the street to her own house.

Doreen tried to stop herself from feeling guilty for leading the woman on, but if the woman was so willing to listen to the dog, then she needed something constructive to keep her busy. Besides, with a bit of luck, when Dozer became accustomed to being picked up and allowed to run free with the other dogs, chances were he would stop howling, anticipating her arrival. Problem solved. She hoped.

For the third time, she walked to Edwin's front door. The barking started again, and in addition to the noise, the door vibrated violently as Dozer jumped up on it repeatedly.

Slowly, she inserted the key and turned it. Behind the door, the frantic Dozer barked one last time, and stopped. The door no longer shook.

Using great caution, Doreen pushed the door open a crack. "Dozer, sit," she commanded.

He didn't. Instead, he squeezed through the opening and leapt at Doreen, his paws landing squarely in her midsection. So much for all her training expertise.

"Dozer, sit," Doreen commanded, pushing him down. To her shock, this time, he did. His tail wagged so hard and fast the whole dog rocked, but he remained sitting. She snapped the leash in her hand onto Dozer's collar and patted him lavishly for his good behavior. Anxious to be on her way, Doreen pulled the door shut and locked it. The discussion with Edwin's neighbor had been a time-consuming distraction, leaving her behind schedule. Fortunately, she made up the time at the rest of her stops.

When she arrived at her property, she released the dogs one by one once the gate was secure. As usual, she played fetch and threw balls and Frisbees to keep them amused, and let them run free.

At the appointed time, she blew the whistle, signaling all the dogs to come. First came the whippet, then the Doberman, and to her shock, next came Dozer with the rest of the smaller dogs trailing far behind.

With the whippet and Doberman both stopped and already sitting, Doreen watched Dozer approach. The closer he got, the more she could tell that he was definitely a city dog. Running full tilt, sticks and dirt flying around him in all directions, when he approached, he did not slow down. At the last possible second, his feet stopped, but the dog was obviously not used to running on a loosely packed surface. He started to slide, but the attempt to regain his balance only made it worse. Before Doreen could move, Dozer crashed into her, knocking her to the ground with a thud, leaving her sitting in the dirt staring at the dogs from eye level.

Dozer circled her, then sat beside the other dogs, his tongue lolling out as he panted furiously. The smaller dogs arrived as Doreen scrambled to her feet. Where did Edwin get this clumsy dog?

She wiped the dust off the seat of her jeans, counted the dogs, and took them home.

&

Doreen heated a can of soup and prepared a salad for supper, eating as she watched television. Tonight, she planned to spend a solitary evening with no one bothering her, no one to keep her company except for Gretchen.

Too tired for her usual Friday night activities, she watched television but couldn't keep her mind on the program. Instead she thought of Edwin, daydreaming about telling him what she thought of his uncontrolled dog. She wondered if he would try to convince her to go out to lunch again before their next scheduled obedience lesson. She knew she would be disappointed if he didn't.

The phone rang when she was up to her elbows in suds, washing her supper dishes. She contemplated letting the answering machine catch it, but didn't want to chance missing a new client.

"Hi, Doreen. It's Friday night."

Edwin. She should have known.

"Yes, it's Friday. So?"

"So let's decide what we're going to do."

"We—?"

"Unless you want to come here."

"Well, no, I—"

"Great. I knew you'd rather I came to visit you, you drive enough in a day. See you in half an hour. Bye." He hung up the phone quickly, not giving her a chance to reply.

Doreen covered her face with one hand as she hung up the phone. He'd done it again.

❧

As she finished the dishes and tidied the kitchen, she wondered if he had anything specific in mind.

Gretchen signaled Edwin's arrival by barking and running to the door exactly half an hour later. Edwin stood in the doorway, tall and handsome, and grinning like a Cheshire cat.

"Hi!" he quipped cheerfully as he stepped inside, playfully scratching Gretchen behind one ear.

Doreen crooked her head to glare at him as he sauntered inside and plopped himself down on the couch. "You knew I'd be too polite to send you away, didn't you?"

He covered his heart with one hand. "You wound me. So, what do you want to do? What do you usually do Friday night?" He patted the couch beside him, then winked.

Doreen stayed standing. She wondered why he was so quick to hang up the phone and get here if he didn't have anything specific in mind. "Most Friday nights I go to church to play volleyball."

Edwin arched his eyebrows. "Church? Volleyball?"

"Yes, volleyball. Haven't you ever played volleyball?"

"Not since high school."

"Well then, you don't know what you're missing."

Narrowing his eyes, he crossed his arms over his chest. He thought he was making himself appear imposing, but the cartoon character in a ridiculous pose on his T-shirt completely undermined his seriousness. "You're joshing me." Knotting his eyebrows, he clamped his lips together, making his lower lip protrude slightly, like a little boy pouting.

Doreen's heart nearly stopped, then started up in double time. She clamped her hands in front of her stomach to stifle the urge to ruffle his hair and run her fingers down his cheeks to soothe him. She cleared her throat. "I'm serious. I do this often on Friday nights."

He cocked his head and narrowed his eyes. "You really do, don't you." It wasn't a question.

"Why don't you believe me? What do you do on Friday nights when you have nothing to do? I'll bet you sit at home all by yourself, don't you?" She glared back, daring him to disagree.

He cowed, shuffling one foot on the ground. "Sometimes," he mumbled.

Doreen crossed her arms and glared back at him to give him a taste of his own medicine. "Sometimes?"

He threw his arms up in the air. "Okay. Most Friday nights! Happy?"

Actually, it didn't make her happy. It made her feel like a shrew for making him admit it out loud.

"I'm not going out to play volleyball with a bunch of kids. I want to do an adult thing. With you."

"Edwin, the kids aren't allowed. This is a late-night thing. It starts at nine."

"No kids? Like, none? At all?"

Finally. It was about time she got through to him. "No kids, no teenagers. This is a young adult thing, for college and careers, and it's a lot of fun. There's been times I've turned down other things because I wanted to go play volleyball." Unable to hold herself back, she strode across the room, stopped inches in front of him, then touched his nose with her forefinger. "Know what? I think you're chicken."

In a flash, Edwin grabbed her wrist, holding it in front of him. "Me? I'm not chicken." His pouty expression changed to a sly grin. "Just scared to death of making a fool of myself."

She smiled, but when his thumb started to massage the underside of her wrist, she yanked her hand away, and moved back a step. "There's a difference?"

The way his expression changed, Doreen didn't dare to ask what the difference was. Instead, she ignored him.

"You can't possibly be any worse than I am. But I just go to have fun. You'll at least have a nice time, and maybe get to meet some new friends."

She glanced up at the clock, then back to Edwin, still stretched out comfortably on her couch. "It doesn't start for an hour. What do you want to do?"

His gaze drifted to her mouth, and his eyes lost their twinkle. As he continued to watch her mouth, Doreen nearly broke out into a cold sweat. "We could go out for coffee," she managed to say in a voice too squeaky to be her own.

"Does that offer include dessert?"

"As long as you're buying."

His eyes finally met hers. His mouth opened as if he were going to reply, but the phone rang, cutting him off. She wasn't sure she wanted to hear what he was going to say.

She tried not to fumble with the phone as she picked it up and answered.

"Oh, hello, Frank. How are you?" She could feel Edwin's eyes digging into her back. She tried to be as brief as possible without being rude. When she finally hung up, her initial impression was correct. Edwin stood across the room, leaning against the wall, his arms crossed over his chest, his mouth drawn to a tight line. This time he wasn't giving her a playful pout. This time he meant it.

"Who was that?" he asked.

"That was Frank."

"Frank who?"

"Would it matter, Edwin? You wouldn't know him anyway."

"What did he want?"

"He wanted to know if I was busy tonight, but I told him I was. Okay?" She didn't want to tell him that Frank was a business client, and he was asking if she could meet him at a breeder's to help select a puppy for a friend. Judging from Edwin's behavior, he looked like he might be a little jealous. Not that it made a difference, there was nothing between them anyway.

"Do you see him often?"

She couldn't believe he had the nerve to ask, but by reflex she answered. "No, I hardly ever see him." She saw him once a month when he paid his bill.

"Good," Edwin mumbled under his breath. "Let's go. And can we take my car?"

nine

As they drove into the dark church parking lot, Doreen recognized a number of the cars, and knew instantly that Edwin would be glad he came tonight.

Walking toward the door with Edwin in tow, Doreen opened her mouth to tell him to stop acting so nervous, but the sudden blast of a car horn beside her nearly sent her into cardiac arrest.

Startled, she screamed and jumped, bumping into Edwin, landing in his arms. Her heart pounded, but she wasn't sure if it was due to fear or proximity. Standing frozen, their eyes locked as his hands settled around her waist. No words were spoken as he neither pushed her away nor removed his hands. Doreen forced herself to breathe. She liked the feel of his arms around her, although she knew she shouldn't.

"Hi, Doreen!" a male voice called out from the car window as it sped into a parking space and screeched to a halt.

Slowly and awkwardly, Doreen disengaged herself from Edwin's grasp, pushed her hair off her brow, then tugged at the hem of her sweater in a futile attempt to calm her shattered nerves.

Edwin stared at the car as the taillights went out. "Who was that?" he demanded, both annoyed at the ignoramus who had just scared them half to death, and amazed at the sensation of touching Doreen, even if only for a fleeting minute.

In the dim lights of the parking lot, he could see a slight

tremor in Doreen's fingers as she toyed with her hair. She sucked in a deep breath, then averted her head. "That's Blair. And if my guess is correct, then Gary will be with him. Come on, I think you'll like them, even after that bad first impression."

As they neared the car, true to her guess, two men got out. Both were tall and in their early twenties, although it was hard to tell if they were good looking in the dark. Edwin wondered why he cared. Doreen was with him tonight.

"Hi, Doll!" the driver called as he waved. "Who's your friend? Want to lose him and come away with me instead?"

Edwin instantly disliked him.

"Hi, Blair," Doreen responded, her voice sounding like Eeyore with her drop in tone. "Dream on."

Both men approached, the passenger holding out his hand to Edwin when they were face-to-face. "Hi, I'm Gary, and the rude guy behind me is Blair."

Doreen rested one hand on Edwin's arm. "Gary, this is my friend Edwin."

"Hi," Edwin said cautiously, shaking hands with both of them, wondering about Doreen's definition of a friend.

A few more cars pulled into the lot as the four of them headed for the building together. Blair's head turned with each new car entering the lot. "Looks like a good crowd tonight. I can hardly wait to get started. I had to miss the last few weeks, and I think I'm getting a little soft. Want to check my muscles, Doreen, and tell me what you think?" He grinned and wiggled his eyebrows at Doreen.

Edwin wanted to punch Blair in the nose.

"Forget it, Blair. Go find someone who wants to be impressed."

Blair elbowed Edwin in the ribs, making Edwin wince.

He gritted his teeth. He would not make a scene.

"Can't blame a guy for trying, eh, Eddie?"

"The name's Edwin."

Blair ignored him and walked faster, his eye on another woman, leaving the group behind. But at least he left Doreen alone.

Doreen shook her head. "Why do you hang around with that loudmouth, Gary?"

Gary snickered. "Hey, someday my dear brother might turn into a decent human being, and maybe someone will want him."

Edwin blinked and tried not to let either Gary or Doreen see him shift his gaze back and forth between the two men. Brothers? In the brief few minutes since they had been introduced, he could plainly see that Blair and Gary were total opposites. Edwin didn't have a brother, and wondered what it would be like.

As they entered the building, he followed Doreen around a couple of corners and down the hall until he found himself in a small gymnasium.

"This is a church, isn't it?" Two volleyball nets stretched above the polished floor, and echoing thuds of bouncing balls resounded off the ceiling. He shook his head. A gym as part of a church? He had never seen anything like it.

Someone tossed a volleyball to Doreen from the open doorway. Bouncing it, she turned her head toward Edwin. "There's more to church than Sunday morning, you know."

"Hi, Doreen!" someone called, but because of the echo, he couldn't tell where the voice originated. Most of the people in attendance were male, most of them in shorts, and a good number of them started that male strut to impress as soon as they noticed Doreen walk in. Edwin fought the urge to put his arm around her and swiped the volleyball instead. Today, he wore jeans, because of all the things he imagined doing with Doreen on a Friday night, meeting a bunch of people in a church gymnasium hadn't even come close. At least he hadn't worn a tie. Next time he would dress more appropriately. He nearly missed the ball as he bounced it. *Next time?*

Another young man approached them. "Good to see you; missed you on Sunday."

Doreen blushed. "I was busy on Sunday." She turned to introduce them. "Dwayne, this is Edwin."

Edwin shook Dwayne's hand. Another friend?

"Everyone's ready to pick teams." Dwayne motioned his hand for them to follow. "Let's go!" He turned and joined the gathering circle.

Doreen stayed close to Edwin as the group divided into four teams, getting ready to play. Everyone respected her unspoken signal to be on the same team as Edwin. He appeared a little out of place, which was perfectly understandable, so she decided to stay close to him until he became more accustomed to the routine.

The volleyball games started, all participants doing very little talking and a lot of laughing. Edwin warmed to the crowd quickly, and true to his sociable nature, found his niche. Doreen noticed, however, that a number of the men who tried to impress her on a regular basis kept an eye on Edwin, as if trying to figure out their relationship. Doreen ignored them as she participated in the game.

Her team won, pitting them against the winner of the game in the other court. Everyone waited in line at the water fountain for the other game to finish, pausing to chat and joke around.

She stood aside to watch a few of the others banter with Edwin. Their effort to include her friend, even though he was a newcomer, warmed her heart.

When the game on the other court finished, they broke up for a few minutes to allow the others to grab a drink, and soon they were back at it, vying for the "championship." Usually, if the games ended early enough, the "champs" bought donuts.

After more hard play, the other team won, but the night was still young, and catcalls of challenge and rematch resounded, resulting in regrouping and another match.

Exhausted but happy, they decided to pack it in just after midnight. Balls bounced off the walls, floors, and a few heads as everyone packed up the nets and balls for the night.

As Edwin helped stack the poles in the storage room, Doreen waited at the water fountain. She turned when she heard Gary's voice behind her.

"Whew," he said in a rush of air, wiping his sleeve on his forehead and pushing his hair back with his hand. "Good game. It always surprises me that someone as short as you can jump so high."

Gary stood in front of her, towering above her small frame. You're six-foot-three. Everyone is short compared to you."

A loud series of clangs from the supply room drowned out her reply. "What?" he shouted.

Another array of noise, followed by shouting then gales of laughter completely obliterated her attempt to repeat herself.

Gary smiled and jerked his head toward the open door, then reached for her hand and led her to continue their conversation in the corridor.

Glancing once over her shoulder for Edwin, Doreen convinced herself that if he ever made it out of the storage room he surely would come find her, so she allowed Gary to escort her out of the gym.

She had known Gary for a long time, having dated him off and on for the past year or so. But, as nice as he was, she had never developed anything more than a friendship as a Christian sister with him. Gary, on the other hand, had a huge crush on her which had not yet been cured, even though she did nothing to encourage him.

As often happened, Gary seemed to be shadowing her all evening, pouncing on the opportunity to chat with her whenever she was alone. Even though he had seen her arrive with Edwin, Gary continued to follow her around. While she found it flattering, she did not want to encourage him when she did not feel the same way. She chatted and joked with him for a while, constantly checking over his shoulder, looking for Edwin.

Finally, unable to stifle a yawn, she tried to excuse herself to find Edwin and go home.

"Sure, Doreen." Gary nodded slowly, then his voice dropped in pitch. "See you Sunday." Before she realized what was happening, he leaned down and brushed a kiss on her cheek and quickly turned and walked away. One hand shot up to cover the cheek he had kissed. She froze, stunned by the unexpected and unsolicited gesture, trying to decide if she should rebuke him for it.

She turned to say something before he disappeared around the corner, but as she turned, the first person she saw was Edwin. Her mouth dropped open, and she whisked her hand behind her back, then to her side. She had nothing to hide. She'd done nothing.

Edwin glared as he strode toward her, his steps uncharacteristically determined. It didn't take a rocket scientist to figure out that he had seen everything. It also didn't take much to see that Edwin was not happy.

"Who is that guy?" he demanded, standing with his feet braced apart and arms folded stiffly across his chest. He turned his head slightly to glare icicles as Gary disappeared down the corridor, then glared back at her.

Doreen blinked at his affront. "What guy?" she asked, stalling to gain some time.

"You know very well what guy. Him!" Edwin jerked his head in the direction of Gary's departure, flopping a lock of damp hair into the center of his forehead. He didn't bother to swish it back.

"That's Gary. You met him in the parking lot."

His eyes narrowed. "Very funny, Doreen. You know what I mean. Who is he?"

Doreen stiffened. "He's a friend."

"What kind of friend?" Edwin demanded, his head lowered almost imperceptibly. "I've never heard you mention his name before."

"He's a good friend. I've known him since we were kids."

"You dating him?"

"We've gone out a few times," she answered honestly, then clamped her lips closed. Why was she allowing him to badger her like this? Who she saw and what she did was none of Edwin's business.

"So you have been out with him. Why won't you go out with me?"

"That's different," she mumbled. Gary had been born and raised a Christian, like she had, but Edwin had not. At that second, she made up her mind. She would not get involved with Edwin while he was maturing in his faith. Besides, she'd known Gary almost all her life. Gary was safe.

"What's he got that I ain't got?"

"I beg your pardon?" Doreen tipped her head to one side. If she didn't know better, she might think that Edwin was jealous.

He bored into her eyes. "What's he like? Describe him."

"Gary? Well, he's intelligent."

"$E = mc^2$." Edwin squared his shoulders, then resettled his arms in their crossed position. "Keep going."

Doreen bit back a smile. Even angry, Edwin couldn't be serious if his life depended on it.

She thought a little more about Gary. As nice as he was, there was nothing about him that excited her, so she decided to state the obvious. "He's good-looking."

Edwin straightened his posture and stiffened, making him appear taller, at the same time he tried to push his messy hair into place.

"Not as good as me." He raised one eyebrow and tipped up one corner of his mouth slightly, no doubt an attempt to look macho. "I'm tall, dark, and handsome. Ask my mother, I'm good-looking like my dad." He stood, waiting for her to continue.

Doreen smiled. Gary was the tallest person she knew. However, except for the fact that she had never seen Edwin's father, she had no argument about the handsome part, in a boyish sort of way. "He comes from a nice family," she continued, baiting him further.

"So do I. You can meet my folks anytime. Just don't ask about Great-Aunt Ethyl. Keep going."

All joking aside, she couldn't help but feel Edwin's competitive edge. "Edwin! What is with you?" she asked, tapping her foot and placing her hands on her hips.

Edwin ignored her. He shuffled his feet wider apart. "What's he like? What's so good about him?" His intimidating stance betrayed the light tone of his voice.

Doreen started to grasp at straws. "He's stable and dependable."

"So am I. I have a good job, I like it, my boss likes me, money's not bad. Keep going."

"He has a nice home."

"My house is nice. I even have a good watchdog."

Doreen tried not to laugh out loud. She couldn't stand it anymore. "The part about the *good* watchdog is debatable."

"Never mind. Keep going. What's so good about this Gary guy?"

She couldn't believe it. Edwin was jealous. "We go to the same church, he's a fellow believer, and I've known him almost all my life."

"I've been to your church," he countered, "and even though I've only been once, and even though I still have a few things to figure and work out, I'm not a total heathen. And I think we're getting to know each other pretty well."

She stared in silence. *This guy is unbelievable.*

"Well?" he asked, lifting his chin slightly, giving him more of an arrogant, aloof appearance, and making her feel shorter.

Doreen looked up. His brown eyes flashed in the bright overhead light of the corridor. "Well, what? What do you want out of me, Edwin?"

In one quick movement, Edwin stepped so close their toes touched. "This," he whispered. Without warning, the fingers of his right hand tipped her chin up, and his left arm circled around her back, pulling her body against his. Slowly, he lowered his head and kissed her gently and tenderly, oblivious to anyone who might have walked by the corridor. Too shocked to protest, as he continued to kiss her, she suddenly decided she didn't want to protest. When they finally separated from what turned out to be a beautiful and sensuous long kiss, Doreen stood breathless.

Taking one step back from him, she had to concentrate on where they were before she could speak. Not only had she allowed him to kiss her when anyone could have walked by, she had thoroughly kissed him back.

Edwin stood stock-still, his face dazed, as if he couldn't believe what he had done.

Doreen glared back, feeling just as stunned. What had passed between them?

His hand slid from her waist to her hand. Gently but firmly, he held on, refusing to let her go. His other large hand tenderly rubbed up and down her forearm. "Well." He sighed, then raised his fingertips to her chin, keeping her gaze locked with his. "I'm not going to say I'm sorry, because I'm not." His mouth curved into the most alluring, warm smile Doreen had ever seen. He winked, making an exaggerated sweep of the corridor with his line of vision proving that no one had seen.

She snapped herself out of her daze, and cleared her throat. "No, I don't suppose you are." As she spoke, she could barely recognize the airy voice she heard as her own. What was happening?

His fingers caressed her chin, his light touch sending pleasant shivers all the way to her toes. Almost painfully slowly, he lifted her face once more as he lowered his head until his lips were almost touching hers. "Are you sorry?" he asked huskily.

Doreen closed her eyes, lost. "No." She parted her lips. He was going to kiss her again, and her knees trembled in anticipation. What was she doing?

Edwin kissed her mouth lightly, nibbled a few kisses to her lower lip, then stopped, giving his mouth enough distance from hers to feel the heat of her lips on his without actually touching. As much as he would have liked to kiss the stuffing out of her, this was neither the time nor the place. Most important, a change had occurred in their relationship, and he needed time to absorb it. His heart pounded as he drifted apart from her. His eyes opened to the sight of Doreen, eyes closed, waiting for more.

He longed to cover her mouth with his, to savor her, to kiss her senseless. But the moment had clearly caught her off guard, and he refused to take advantage. This was not something Doreen would take lightly. For that matter, neither did he take it lightly. How would she feel tomorrow? How would she feel in an hour?

He had to create some distance, but not let her get too far away. He needed to let her regroup. He needed to let himself regroup, but he didn't want to be separated from her. Not yet. Instead of doing what he wanted, he released her completely. He had to be with her, but not let himself touch her. "I'm starving. Feel like pizza?"

Doreen opened her eyes and blinked dumbly up at him. He was thinking of food? Her world nearly spun off its axis, wanting him to kiss her again, and he wanted pizza? Her ego plummeted down somewhere into her shoes. All she could do was nod, completely at a loss for any better response.

Edwin grabbed her hand and proceeded to lead her out the door without pausing to say good-bye to anyone. She didn't have the presence of mind to do anything other than follow him to his car.

ಸಿ

By the time they entered the late-night pizza establishment, Doreen managed to clear her head. No matter how she felt, no matter how confused, she refused to make a fool of herself. Casual relationships were not her style, and casual was all Edwin would ever be. She lived her life, to the best of her ability, to honor and serve God. She had no time for frivolity or foolishness. Although she enjoyed herself as much as the next person, she had a focus in her life, and he didn't. Before she left him for the evening, she planned to tell him so.

She never got the chance. Edwin kept the conversation lighthearted and casual. Every time she tried to change the subject to more serious matters, he came out with a comment so far out of left field she didn't know how to respond. Finally, she gave up and let him talk, telling her stories of his life and friends. At first she let him prattle on, but before she knew it, he had her joining in and bantering back with him.

Against her better judgment, she enjoyed his company, and time passed quickly. Before she knew it, it was three o'clock in the morning. She hadn't known there was an all-night pizza restaurant in town. Now she knew. She didn't even notice that Edwin knew all the staff.

By the time Edwin dropped her off at her door, she greeted a very sleepy Gretchen. Edwin followed her into the house, made sure everything was safe and secure, then left quietly.

Doreen waved through the window as he drove away, allowing the events of the evening to come back to her mind with astute clarity. She also thought back to the day she had first met Edwin at Bill's pet shop, how cute and endearing he was when his dog embarrassed him so badly at the store. Then she thought of his first awkward phone call, the first time they went out, and how things had changed.

For a guy who didn't have a serious bone in his body, this relationship was getting far deeper than she could have anticipated.

As she changed into her pajamas and went into the washroom to brush her teeth, thoughts of Edwin still raced through her mind. She stared back at her wide-eyed reflection in the mirror. She couldn't get thoughts of Edwin out of her head.

She rested her hands on the edges of the sink, closed her eyes, and lowered her head to pray.

Lord what is happening? I'm so confused. I feel called to be with Edwin, to help him develop a relationship with You, yet here I am, falling in love with him.

Her head shot up as she gasped out loud. Was she falling in love with him? Doreen covered her face with her hands and lowered her forehead to touch the edge of the sink. It was too late to deny it. She had fallen for his charm, his easy manner, his open sincerity, and fallen badly. But that was impossible. She couldn't take the man seriously at all. He was sloppy, undisciplined, he always said exactly what he felt no matter what, and he treated everything so lightly.

Raising her head, she looked at her somber reflection in the mirror once more. She could almost feel the heat of his lips on hers. He was a great kisser. Her eyes shut again as the force of realization hit her. Edwin!

How did he feel about her? She really didn't know. While obviously flirting with her, he also flirted, although to a lesser degree, with almost every woman who paid him any attention. While he seemed to want to spend time with her, he had never done anything else that would suggest anything other than sharing a fun evening together. And now this! After he kissed her like that, her head had spun. For a while, she thought he was actually jealous of Gary.

Now she realized he was just carrying a joke past its fore-gone conclusion—so typical of Edwin.

Her watch beeped the hour, indicating four o'clock, the latest she had ever been out.

More thoughts of Edwin tumbled through her brain, each question posing conflicting answers. She rubbed her eyes. The reason she wasn't thinking straight must be because she was exhausted. It had to be. She certainly did not love the man. He was all wrong for her. He didn't know her Savior. Besides, falling in love was supposed to make you happy. Doreen did not feel happy.

Carelessly, she threw her toothbrush back into the holder and crawled off to bed, knowing that it would still be a while before she fell asleep.

ten

Doreen opened one eye, trying to determine the origin of a horrid scraping sound, somewhat akin to fingernails on a chalkboard. When a single bark followed more scraping, both eyes sprang open. Gretchen scratched at the bedroom door again, signaling her need to go outside. Doreen bolted to a sitting position and jumped out of bed. Gretchen never woke her to go outside unless she was about to be sick.

With the sudden change from sleep to running came a wave of dizziness. She staggered to the door, opened it, then supported herself in the doorway to watch Gretchen make a beeline to the doggie door.

Doreen blinked the fuzziness out of her head. If Gretchen hadn't been sick, why had she needed to go out so badly? As she passed the living room on her way back to bed, she stopped dead at the time showing on the VCR. She blinked, rubbed her eyes, and checked again, just to be sure. It was nearly noon.

This was Edwin's fault.

Her stomach grumbled, but she didn't know whether to respond with lunch or breakfast. She chose the quickest. Breakfast.

As she rinsed her cereal bowl and placed it in the dishwasher, she thought more about the night before. In all fairness she couldn't blame Edwin; what had happened was no one's fault but her own. She had invited Edwin to volleyball, and she had the choice to go out for a snack or come home. Even then, no one forced her to stay until such a late hour. Truthfully, she thoroughly enjoyed listening to him tell his tall tales. And if she'd lain in bed for hours staring at the ceiling, she had no one to blame but herself.

At the stroke of noon, the phone rang. "Hi, Edwin," she answered without waiting for a voice.

For a moment, pure silence hung on the line. "How'd you know it was me?" came the mumbled reply.

"I just knew." She giggled.

"Oh. Are we still on for our obedience lesson?"

"Sure, I think I can teach you a thing or two about obedience. Your dog can come too." She giggled again.

Again, silence echoed on the line. "Doreen? Is everything okay?"

"Just fine. Why do you ask?"

"Never mind. Have you had lunch?"

Doreen checked the clock on the wall, shaking her head. She still couldn't believe it. "Are you kidding? I've barely finished breakfast."

"I know. Me too. I'm not even sure I'm awake yet. I never realized that playing volleyball was such hard work."

She opened her mouth to respond, but Dozer's sharp bark came over the phone loud enough for her to hold the receiver away from her ear. Following that came a clattering and scrambling as Edwin fumbled with the phone.

"Hey, listen Doreen, I've gotta go. Dozer knows I'm ready to leave and he's driving me nuts. See you in half an hour. Bye."

She barely had time to mumble her good-bye before the dial tone buzzed in her ear. One day she would figure out how he did that.

❧

Half an hour. Half an hour? With a frantic groan she dashed into the washroom to shower. As she hurriedly washed her hair, her mind began to race. How would he greet her? How would she greet him? Had things really changed? The man had kissed her. So what if she'd almost melted into a little puddle on the floor. It had obviously not been a very earthmoving experience for him if his first thought afterward was pizza. Obviously she hadn't captivated him. The thought stung, but what was happening between them?

Certainly she meant more to him than merely a mealtime companion, or an obedience trainer for his dog. For the most part, she'd been quite reluctant, yet he kept calling. At times, he really knew how to turn on the charm, but maybe he always behaved this way with women. What if he wasn't treating her any differently? Then she was ten times the fool.

She scrambled into jeans and a blouse and pulled her hair back in a rubber band to dry. She had just walked into the kitchen, and was thinking about starting some coffee, when Gretchen barked and ran to the door.

Curiosity got the better of her, and Doreen peeked through the curtains, to see whether Edwin would try another impressive demonstration with Dozer. Only this time, she hoped he would let the dog out of the car first.

Edwin exited the car empty-handed. Dozer hopped out behind him, but before the dog ran to the door Edwin honked Dozer's nose and walked away, leaving the dog sitting impatiently beside the car.

Dying to see what would happen, Doreen opened the door and stepped onto the porch, with Gretchen waiting beside her.

Edwin walked up the path, nodded, winked, and strode past her into the house without speaking. Doreen also didn't speak as he continued into her office, then ducked behind the door.

"Dozer, come!" he called, and was silent.

Dozer came. He ran to her, stopped, looked around, and then plowed past her. Up to the challenge to find his missing master, he ran into the living room, sniffing the air as he loped along. He ran into the kitchen, checked under the table, then started eagerly checking the other rooms.

However, it would have been more of a challenge if Edwin hadn't started to snicker. Once Edwin started laughing, it took Dozer exactly ten seconds to find him, hunkered down behind the door.

"Good boy!" he praised his dog, patting him proudly. Edwin raised his head, peering up at Doreen from his cramped position on the floor. "Well? What do you think? Great, isn't he?"

"I suppose," Doreen said weakly, unable to evaluate the performance until she determined if this was a genuine training exercise or a game.

Edwin grinned. "Got a cookie for him?"

"A cookie? I don't give cookies to dogs, it's bad for them. I've got plenty of dog biscuits, though."

"That's what I meant."

"He's a dog, they're not called cookies."

He ruffled Dozer's ears and kissed him smack in the middle of his big, black, wet nose. "He's my friend, and they're cookies."

Doreen's stomach churned. "He's a dog, and he's a pet."

Dozer licked Edwin on the mouth. Doreen covered her mouth with her hand. She had kissed that mouth? Edwin merely laughed while her face turned green.

She glared down at him. "You are so exasperating!"

He waggled his eyebrows at her. "You're so cute."

Silence dragged; the only sound in the room was Dozer's panting. As Doreen continued to glower down at him,

Edwin hugged Dozer from his position on the floor, and two sets of brown eyes stared up at her. If she hadn't been so annoyed, she might have been amused. Maybe.

Remembering one of the reasons she had anticipated his visit, Doreen stomped into the living room. Behind her, Edwin cleared his throat, muffling the sound of what she knew was him trying not to laugh as he followed her.

"I've got something for you," she grumbled.

"For me?"

"Here." She picked up her Bible from the coffee table and thrust it into his stomach, suddenly ashamed of her huffy mood when giving him something so important.

He held it reverently with both hands and stared at the leather cover. Head bowed, he lightly grazed the embossed gold lettering with his fingertips, then clutched it to his chest. "Wow. Thanks."

"You're welcome," she said, softening at his sudden change in demeanor.

"I think I promised to read the whole thing, didn't I?"

She nodded. All her irritation dissolved as Edwin became thoughtful and opened the Bible. He read a few words, flipped to another section, rested his finger on one of the highlighted verses and read a little more. His brows knotted and his lips moved as his finger rested on one of the longer, complicated Old Testament names.

He closed the Bible, grasping it tightly shut with both hands. "I'm probably going to need help reading it, you know."

"You're a big boy. Read it yourself."

"Very funny." For once, he didn't smile. "I meant, I'll probably have a million questions, and I was hoping you could help me with the answers."

"I'll do what I can, and if you have anything I can't

answer, I'll find someone who can. If you want, you can come with me to a Bible study once a week."

"Bible study? I don't want to go to school to study it, I only want to read it and ask a few questions."

She found his inexperience rather refreshing. "No, it isn't like school. I go to Bible study on Tuesday evenings. It's an informal group, and we meet every week at the same house. We take turns picking a topic, one a week, and see what the Bible says about it. Anyone is welcome."

"Even me? I've only been to your church once."

"Especially you." She would never have believed that inviting a new Christian or an unbeliever to Bible study could be this easy.

"Well. . .I don't know."

"We have cake and coffee afterwards."

He grinned ear to ear. "What time shall I pick you up?"

She knew that would do it. "It's only a few blocks from your house, actually. I can either pick you up on my way, or leave my van at your house."

She watched his smile fade, then brighten. She would never forget his silly plan to waylay her van the day she had joined him for dinner after the Baldwin's wedding.

"Okay, I'm new at this, but why would you go to a Bible study? Doesn't the pastor tell you everything you need to know? And how is this going to help me to know God better?"

"Say you have a question the pastor doesn't address Sunday morning. What would you do, wait Sunday after Sunday, hoping it will come up, or take a few minutes and look it up yourself?"

"I think you know the answer to that, I mean, since you put it that way. Okay, I get it."

"And don't be afraid to pray. Prayer is simply talking to

God, and sometimes you might be surprised at the way God answers prayers."

"You make it sound so easy, but if that's all there is to it, I trust you."

"Go at your own speed, and remember, you're not alone."

He nodded. It was true. He wasn't alone. And praying really wasn't so hard. Over the past week, he'd thought a lot about the pastor's words explaining God's commitment to His children. He'd been happy and content rolling through life until a few weeks ago.

Nothing had changed, not even the smallest detail, yet a little voice deep down that he'd never heard before kept nagging him that something was indeed missing. It was time to quit drifting, but his life held no paths to even choose from. His life was an open field, and he was running in circles in the middle of it. Then he met Doreen.

He thought if he could earn her affection, then he would be a happy man.

She was weakening, he knew it. She hadn't turned him down without a good reason so far, although he tried his best not to give her the opportunity. And when he kissed her and she kissed him back, he thought he'd died and gone to heaven. But still, it wasn't enough. He'd lain in bed all night staring at the dark ceiling, thinking.

All night his thoughts had drifted between visions of Doreen with her eyes closed and her lips moist from his kisses, and thoughts of still being alone. He'd talked to God. He didn't know what to say, but his thoughts seemed to tumble out, and in doing so, he knew God was listening. And he knew God cared.

And now he was going to learn more about God. With Doreen's help. He hugged her Bible like a teddy bear.

"There's another reason I wanted to talk to you, Edwin."

Edwin cringed. It sounded like a confession was coming, and he didn't think he wanted to hear it.

"What?" he asked, steeling his nerve to take it like a man.

"I think I started something with your neighbor."

"Neighbor?" She wanted to talk about Mrs. Primline? He tried not to be too relieved. He'd almost thought she was going to tell him she didn't want to see him anymore. He couldn't take that. Not now. Not ever.

"Yes, Mrs. Primline, that elderly lady you told me about who's been giving you a hard time about Dozer. I think I kind of gave her the wrong impression."

He shook his head back and forth so fast a lock of hair flopped onto his forehead. "What are you talking about?"

Her face turned red, and she lowered her head to stare at her feet, then rubbed one toe on the floor. "Don't be surprised if you see her lurking around your house."

"Pardon me?"

"I think I led her to believe that I was some sort of canine behavioral expert, and now she's going to study your dog's howling, expecting me to tell her what's wrong with him."

"There's nothing wrong with him."

"That's a matter of opinion."

He was about to rebuke her, but in the few seconds it took for him to think of what to say, they both heard the splashing of Dozer drinking out of the toilet as Gretchen drank daintily from her bowl. Doreen's eyes narrowed as she scowled at him, but she didn't comment. Both dogs disappeared out the doggie door in search of more adventure, but not before Dozer tripped on his way through the opening.

"I think I let her believe that once I analyze the dog's

howls, I'll be able to stop him."

"Don't worry about it. He's really not that bad, anyway. She tends to exaggerate." A few times he'd listened to her talk about her wonderful grandchildren. Child prodigies, all seven of them.

"I didn't mean to mislead her, but I didn't know what to say to her."

"I doubt that she will take you seriously. Don't worry, she'll forget all about it."

"I don't know. . ."

"Forget about it, Doreen. The dogs are already outside. Let's carry on with the obedience lesson, before we lose them out there."

૨**

Edwin grinned as he patted Dozer on the rump. Doreen was right. With a little time and effort, the dog really was eager to learn. She freely admitted that, on every lesson, they covered more than she usually did with most dogs. With more than enough to practice, the lesson was over.

"Free for supper?" he asked.

Doreen checked her watch, then shrugged her shoulders. "I guess so," she mumbled. He would never understand her apparent indecision every time he asked for her company. But then if she ever agreed with any enthusiasm, he would probably faint. "Just don't say we'll order pizza!"

"Why? Don't they deliver out here in the wilderness?" He ducked as she halfheartedly threw a stick at him. He would have liked to tumble her down into the leaves on the ground and kiss the stuffing out of her again, but instead, he broke the stick into little pieces and threw it up into the air.

"I'd rather cook. I have to get up early tomorrow morning for the first service, so it can't be a late night."

"Don't go through too much trouble," Edwin said, raising his finger as a warning. "I don't want you to go to any extra effort just for me. You'll make me overridden with guilt, and I couldn't handle that."

"I'll dig something out of the freezer and make it nice and simple."

"Sounds kinda domestic." She smacked him lightly on the forearm with the leash, then strutted to the house with her nose up in the air.

He couldn't believe it. A woman cooking him dinner. Wait till he told his mother about this. She'd be ready to order the wedding invitations.

Edwin volunteered to help, not that he would be of much use except for pressing the buttons on the microwave, but he wanted to be with Doreen and enjoy the informal atmosphere.

He never knew that making a meal could be so much fun. Before he knew it, a nutritious dinner was cooked and on the table. This time, he followed Doreen's example before they ate. He bowed his head and listened carefully as she said a short prayer asking God to bless the meal they had prepared together, then answered her "amen" with one of his own. Sharing a prayer in the quiet kitchen without the crowd of her church friends or the noise and chatter of the restaurant around them lent a quiet intimacy to their time together. He treasured it.

They were both so hungry they ate the meal with very little conversation. "You know why this is so good?" she asked, dabbing the corner of her mouth with her napkin.

He shook his head, wondering if she'd felt the same bond growing between them.

"Because we missed lunch."

He laughed, then insisted on doing the dishes to repay

her for cooking, but Doreen insisted on drying. Usually a chore he left until he needed something again, today washing dishes turned into a pleasant experience. Through constant banter and much laughter, Edwin was almost sorry when the last pot was dried and put in its place.

They moved to the living room to talk, and at first he felt guilty trying to stifle the frequent urge to yawn. Soon he noticed Doreen having the same problem. He decided to make a graceful exit.

Pausing to say good night at the door, Edwin stepped up close to Doreen. More than ever, he wanted to kiss her properly. Tonight was a first for him, a quiet intimate evening at home, an evening he'd never forget. He'd quietly enjoyed her company, no pressure, and in the quiet of her home, he hadn't felt the need to impress. As far as he could tell, she also enjoyed herself. He didn't want to blow the end of a perfect day.

"So, see you at church tomorrow?"

"Sure, I'm not hard to find."

Edwin smiled and gently brushed his fingertips along the soft skin of her cheek. He wondered if she could feel his hand shaking, so he withdrew it to avoid looking like an nervous teenager. Kissing her in the heated moment of a fit of jealousy was one thing, but now that they were alone in the dark, the pressure mounted. Worse than his own nervousness, he couldn't tell what she was thinking.

"I'll be listening. Playing any songs I know?"

"Probably not. You've got to come a number of times before the songs become familiar."

Edwin tucked Doreen's Bible under his arm and rammed his hands in his pockets, trying hard not to shuffle his feet. "Then soon they will be familiar. See you tomorrow."

Abruptly, he turned and walked to his car. As he opened

the car for Dozer to jump in, the word "coward" kept echoing in his brain.

&

The music flowed from Doreen's fingers as the piano sang beneath her touch. Her mind filled with praise and worship as the band and congregation joined together in joyful song to God's glory.

Instead of listening to the pastor's message, Doreen and the other members of the worship team slipped out for coffee and a donut. They would hear the same sermon during the second service. Doreen did not want to appear bored hearing it for a second time when she sat with Edwin. The group of them returned with plenty of time to spare.

The second service did not go well. Knowing Edwin was sitting out there somewhere, Doreen couldn't concentrate. Nothing flowed as it had earlier in the morning. She struggled with every song and had to force herself to narrow her focus in order to keep together with the band.

Her hands were shaking by the time the worship leader completed the final prayer before the pastor's message. When the rest of the worship team joined their families, Doreen sat with Edwin.

She found him in the same spot as the week before. He silently nodded a greeting as she slipped into the empty seat beside him. Listening intently to the pastor, Edwin did not once turn in her direction, and to her disappointment, he did not hold her hand as she hoped he would. Part of the reason she couldn't concentrate on the piano was the anticipation of the possibility that he would. It looked like the thought had not even entered his mind. Crushed, Doreen turned her attention to the pastor's message, where it should have been in the first place.

The topic was an extension from the week before, about

Christian living, and living life as a Christian every day instead of Sundays only. Edwin sat stiffly, listening, his attention never wavering. He didn't even look at Doreen.

As they did at every service, the entire worship team quietly slipped to the front for the closing hymn and prayer. Doreen glanced at Edwin, but he appeared lost in thought and didn't seem to notice when she left the pew. This morning, instead of his usual closing remarks, the pastor quoted Matthew 4:19 and 20, where Jesus called Simon and Andrew to leave their nets and become fishers of men. The pastor then called anyone who wanted to commit their lives to Jesus Christ to step forward.

The band began to play a low-key accompaniment as the pastor waited for a response. About halfway through the song, Doreen glanced over to see what Edwin was doing.

He wasn't in his seat. Just then, Doreen noticed that he was standing at the front, his eyes closed, head bowed, with the pastor's hand on one of his shoulders. Doreen almost stopped playing as she watched the pastor and Edwin praying together.

At the final chord, Doreen bolted from the front platform to join Edwin as he returned to his seat to collect their belongings. She didn't know what to say, so she said nothing. Edwin had just responded to an altar call, to openly commit himself to following Jesus. Without her. Lost in thought, she jumped when he spoke.

"You live like that. Every day your faith in God is apparent in everything you do. You're such a good example for me, Doreen, I'm grateful to have a friend like you."

Doreen smiled sweetly, but her stomach suddenly went to war with itself. Friend? That was it? He considered her merely a friend?

"Thanks, I'm glad." Her words sounded hollow, even to

her own ears. "Are we going to join the group for lunch?" she asked, although at the moment, eating was the last thing she wanted to do.

"To tell the truth, I don't feel very sociable right now. Do you mind?"

Her stomach dove into her toes. He wanted to be alone.

"That's okay," she mumbled, trying to force a smile. If he didn't want her company, she would swallow her pride and give him an easy way out. "Guess I'll see you later." Instead of joining the usual crowd, she would go quietly home alone, and be miserable.

Narrowing his eyes, Edwin tried to guess what she was thinking, and what she meant by "later." Did she mean later, as in after lunch, or later, as in the brush-off? His already shaky level of confidence plummeted to rock-bottom that she would rather go out with her friends from church than with him.

He swallowed his pride and refused to give up. "Will I see you at the evening service? I really wanted to ask you a few questions." He patted his Bible, the one she had loaned him, which lay next to him on the pew. He'd done a bit of random reading before he'd left the house and shoved every scrap of paper he could find in the places where he had a question. "I feel kinda stupid asking some of these things in front of a large group, and I was hoping we could go somewhere to be alone."

"Alone?" Her voice sounded mousy, not like Doreen at all. "With me?"

He wondered if she felt sick or something. He'd noticed that her piano playing didn't have the same flare as it had last week. He swallowed to clear his throat. "It's okay, if you're not hungry we can go through the drive-thru and I'll get something quick for myself, or I can make a sandwich at my house. But if you don't mind watching me eat, I wanted to talk to you without interruption from well-meaning but unwelcome parties." He paused as he gathered his courage, then picked up one of her hands, which was freezing cold. He rubbed it with both of his hands. "And," he stated with emphasis, "I want to spend the rest of the day with you, too." He smiled, hoping what he lacked in charm he made up for with honesty.

Doreen opened her eyes wide and stared at him. He was holding onto her left hand for dear life. She nodded, and he led her outside to his car.

He was determined to take good care of her until she felt better.

eleven

On Tuesday, before she turned into Edwin's driveway, Doreen cautiously checked the house across the street for any signs of activity. She'd been picking Dozer up for nearly a week, and although Edwin had warned her that Mrs. Primline could be a nuisance, she'd only met her once. She found it difficult to believe that her plan about spying on the dog had worked, but she hadn't seen the woman since that day.

Monday had gone by without incident, although nothing could have fazed her on Monday. After the service, when she realized that Edwin had wanted to forgo the usual crowd in order to be alone with her, her appetite had returned and they had found a quiet corner in a restaurant where she had never been. They had stayed so long they were nearly late for the evening service.

All his questions had been good and valid, well thought out, proving he took everything he read seriously.

Throughout the entire day Monday, she had either pondered his comments or daydreamed about the way he treated her on Sunday. When she'd finally convinced him that she was indeed hungry, he'd sat beside her in the restaurant instead of across the table, and except for the nature of their discussion, he'd been almost romantic.

He had followed her home, claiming he wanted to make sure she arrived safely. She assumed it was to kiss her good-bye in private, but when the final moment came and his fingertips brushed her cheek, he had rested his hand on her forehead, made a lame joke about her being not so hot, and hadn't kissed her at all.

Monday evening they had spent hours on the phone with more questions and answers. She had done her best to answer everything he threw at her. When his questions had been exhausted, he kept her entertained with more funny stories and general conversation, until she had realized it was long past her bedtime.

When she had arrived home Tuesday, she found a long message on her answering machine from Edwin. He had been reading his Bible on his lunch break, and had a question that he wanted answered immediately.

Soon he would either run out of questions, or she'd have to call in for reinforcements. Unfortunately, he missed Bible study Tuesday night due to unexpected overtime.

❧

Wednesday morning, Doreen managed to open Edwin's front door and snap Dozer on the leash without incident, but as soon as she walked outside, she saw Mrs. Primline running across the road, straight for her.

"Yoo Hooooooo!!!!! Miss Dog Lady!!!!" she called as she ran, waving one hand jerkily in the air. "Wait!"

Doreen opened the rear of the van, secured Dozer in his travel kennel, then turned to face Edwin's neighbor. "Good morning, Mrs. Primline. How are you today?"

Mrs. Primline waved something small and black in the air. "I did it! I taped that animal, and he didn't know I was there." She thrust a cassette tape into Doreen's hand, then wrapped her wrinkled fingers around Doreen's hand and pressed Doreen's fingers around the tape.

Doreen stared at the tape in her hand. The woman had done it. Now she had no choice but to respond. She leaned into the van and popped the tape into the cassette player, pressed the play button, and waited.

A horrible howl exploded from the speakers, long and melancholy, and very, very loud.

Doreen covered her mouth with her hands. "Does he always sound like that?" she gasped, unable to believe what she was hearing. She couldn't imagine the entire neighborhood having to put up with hours of this madness.

"No, usually he holds the high part at the end for longer, but I fear he may have heard me. Do you need to hear more? He started again after a few minutes if you fast forward the tape. And I have another tape at home."

Doreen cleared her throat. "Do you mind if I borrow this tape?"

The little woman patted Doreen on the shoulder. "I made it for you, dearie. Just like you asked. Can you tell what his problem is?"

"Well, he's not in pain, ma'am, but he is very sad and lonely. Has he been any different since I've been taking him?"

Nodding, Mrs. Primline handed her the empty case for the cassette. "Yes, now he howls when you leave too."

Doreen cringed. She had made him worse, not better. But Bulldozer wasn't really a bad dog, only poorly trained, undisciplined, clumsy, loud, and annoying. But he exhibited great potential.

"Thanks for your help, I'll see what I can figure out."

"Oh!" Mrs. Primline beamed. "You're quite welcome, young lady. And tell me, is Eddie going to visit you again this evening? Tonight is Bulldozer's little doggie class, isn't it?"

As if being called the dog lady wasn't bad enough, now she ran "little doggie classes." She also wondered exactly how much Edwin told his neighbor. "Yes, but I'm not sure if he's coming yet. Why?" She wondered if Edwin knew that his neighbor watched his coming and going.

"My bridge club is meeting tonight, and Annabelle made some of Eddie's favorite cookies, so she wants to know if he'll be home." She leaned closer to Doreen. "I think Annabelle likes dear Eddie. Dorothy does, too."

The neighborhood grandmothers baked him cookies? It didn't surprise her that little old ladies might want to look after him.

She checked her watch. "I'm sorry, I really have to go, but I'm sure I'll see you around another time." Doreen opened the van door. In fact, she was sure she would see Mrs. Primline again, and again, and again.

&

Impatiently counting the rings, Doreen waited for Edwin to answer his phone. It was past seven, and she wondered where he was, and why his new answering machine wasn't on.

She was about to hang up, when he finally answered, panting. No sooner had she asked whether he was coming over, but he cut her off, saying he would be right there.

He arrived in half an hour flat.

She waited in the doorway as he called Dozer to heel and led him into the house. "Before the obedience lesson, we have to talk."

Doreen stood to the side as he kicked off his shoes, almost walked away, then turned to straighten them and place them neatly against the wall. "I don't know how to tell you this, but I think I made you miss out on a treat," Doreen said, watching him.

"Oh?" He sauntered to her couch and flopped down onto it.

"Yes, Mrs. Primline told me her friend Annabelle made

you some cookies. She said they were your favorite."

"You mean I missed them? She makes the best cookies I've ever tasted." He made a big circle using both hands, joining both index fingers and both thumbs. "They're loaded with chocolate and pecans and they're this big!" He closed his eyes and sighed.

"I guess the ladies will eat them for you. She said something about bridge night." Doreen giggled.

"We gotta go." Edwin jumped to his feet and started to put his shoes back on.

"Edwin?"

He reached over and grabbed Doreen by the wrist. "Quick! Maybe there's some left!"

"What are you doing?" she protested to no avail.

"We can do the obedience lesson at my house, and we can talk in the car as well as we can in your living room, with the exception that, at my house, the best cookies in the world are waiting."

"Now, wait," she complained, trying to pull back. "She said they were for you."

"They always give me six, but the little henhouse group has been watching you, and I'll bet they've brought extra this time." He pulled on her arm. "Come on, Doreen, time's a wasting."

"Wait! I don't have my shoes on!"

Edwin let her go, barely giving her enough time to slip on her sneakers. She locked both dogs in the house, then ran to the car with her shoes untied. She barely had her seatbelt fastened before he took off in a puff of dust and sped down the gravel driveway.

"You said you wanted to talk. So talk." Edwin kept his eyes on the road, but appeared jubilant at his victory in getting her out of the house.

"You realize that Mrs. Primline approached me."

"Of course, or you wouldn't have known about the cookies."

"Your dog's howling should embarrass you, you know."

"Aw, come on, Doreen, he's not that bad."

Doreen pulled the tape out of her purse, popped it into Edwin's tape deck, and hit the play button. Mournful howling filled the car, the low tones rising in a despondent crescendo, enriched fully by Edwin's stereo system.

"What in the world is that awful noise!" Edwin exclaimed as he shifted gears around the bend in the road. "Turn it off! There's something wrong with my stereo!"

"That's your dog."

"No way."

"I'm afraid so. Mrs. Primline gave me this tape today."

"No wonder she accuses me of torturing him. What am I going to do?"

"And that's not all. I'm afraid I've made him worse, because now he not only howls for an hour after you leave, he howls for another hour after I leave."

"Great."

Mrs. Primline's second sample boomed from the speaker. Dozer's low rumble rose to a sorrowful pitch, peaking as he sustained the high note at the end of his lamenting aria. The tweeters in the speakers rattled.

"We'll have to make sure he isn't left alone."

We? How did I get involved? "Bright idea," Doreen replied sarcastically. "Now how would *we* go about such a thing?"

He lowered his voice. "We can't leave him alone, so we'll have to get married."

Doreen glowered in silence. Leave it to Edwin to be cavalier about marriage. Marriage was a serious commitment made before God and man, till death do you part. Last week she'd been foolish enough to think she might be falling in love with Edwin, but he obviously didn't take anything seriously. To be so frivolous with the topic of marriage was not funny. She was insulted.

"How dare you!" She smacked him on the arm. With both hands on the wheel, he was unable to defend himself.

"Hey! Cut it out!" He leaned away but couldn't avoid a second swat. "I was only joking!"

"That's the problem, and I don't think you're very funny."

"Chill out!"

Doreen pushed herself into the back of her seat, fuming. She crossed her arms and stared out the window. Why was she so angry? Lots of couples joked about getting married, didn't they? But she and Edwin were not a couple. What were they? She couldn't even look at him as she spoke. "How dare you suggest we get married because of a dog."

"Well, it's not like I'm suggesting we get married because you're pregnant."

"What!" she screamed, and then fell pointedly silent.

Edwin's voice lowered to a mumbled whisper. "Why do I have the feeling I said the wrong thing?"

Doreen maintained her grim silence for the rest of the trip.

"Would it help if I said I was sorry?" Edwin asked as he pulled into his driveway.

Doreen gritted her teeth. All her life, she'd been taught to forgive, but she'd never felt less like doing so. "Never mind. I'm probably overreacting."

"I'm sorry," he said plainly and simply.

They were no sooner out of the car when a swarm of elderly ladies descended upon them.

Doreen painted a smile on her face, forcing herself to be sociable as Mrs. Primline introduced her as Eddie's new lady friend. She would have preferred to be called the dog lady. The ladies ushered them across the street into Mrs. Primline's house, and presented them with a huge plate of giant-sized, mouthwatering cookies.

Doreen politely accepted one cookie. When she bit into it, she knew why Edwin had dragged her on the long drive. They were worth every mile. By the time she started on her second cookie, Edwin had nearly finished his third.

While they ate, the ladies surrounded them with animated discussion. Doreen cringed when Annabelle started showing off photographs of her new baby granddaughter. Annabelle glanced at Edwin and Doreen with one eye narrowed and smiled.

Fortunately, Mrs. Primline chose that moment to drag them into the backyard to see her prize rosebush. As Mrs. Primline was beginning to explain at length her new method of controlling aphids, the phone rang. She excused herself, leaving Edwin and Doreen alone in the twilight.

As the two stood in awkward silence, Edwin's arm brushed Doreen's, and his hand closed over her shoulder as he turned her to face him. "I think we just had our first fight. Still mad at me?"

After watching his gracious behavior with the "henhouse group," as he called them, Doreen noticed how he charmed them all. She had to admit that he had charmed her as well. She smiled and shook her head.

"Good. Then this is where we kiss and make up."

Without waiting for a response, he tilted her chin so that she stared up into his eyes. Backlit by the faint glow of the moon and the distant glimmer of the street lamp, his eyes shimmered. The earthy fragrance of the roses created an aura of romance. She couldn't pull away. Slowly, Edwin's head lowered until his lips were almost touching hers.

"This is the best part about fighting." When he spoke, she could feel the movement against her lips. Not giving her a chance to protest, his mouth covered hers.

He kissed her gently and tenderly, then more passionately as he pulled her body against his. All she could do was drape her arms behind his neck and kiss him back. Warm and solid, he clung almost desperately to her. She really had no intention of running away.

At the sound of a loud burst of laughter from inside the house, Edwin broke away, struggling for breath. He couldn't believe what he'd just done, and right there in Mrs. Primline's rose garden.

Under other circumstances, it might have been romantic, but tonight, it was plain foolishness. What if one of the old ladies had seen them? Doreen would have died of embarrassment, destroying any chances of moving forward with their relationship.

Slowly, he ran his fingers against the softness of her cheek. With both hands, he cupped her face, brushing his thumbs against her temples. Her eyes fluttered open, glittering in the near darkness. She was beautiful, radiant.

"Let's get outta here," he mumbled with a voice so low and husky he barely recognized it as his own.

They never made it back to Edwin's house. By the time they were able to politely but firmly disentangle themselves from the grandmothers, it was nearly Doreen's bedtime, so Edwin drove her home.

Although conversation was stilted at first, things quickly livened up as they discussed various options and methods to soothe Dozer. They decided that Edwin should leave the radio on whenever he had to leave, so that Dozer would hear voices.

The trip ended too soon. While she fumbled with the key

in the lock, he had to touch her. He rested his fingertips, and then his palm on her shoulder. Before she could turn the key, his other hand found its way to her waist. She pushed the door open, and both dogs bounded out, running in circles around their legs.

As the dogs swirled around them, Edwin pulled Doreen next to him so her back nestled against his stomach. She felt good. Too good. When she turned her head to the side and tipped her chin to look up at him, he couldn't stand it any longer. If he kissed her now he wouldn't be able to stop. Instead, he tilted his head and kissed the delicate wisps at the edge of her forehead, the closest he could come without losing control of himself.

"Good night, Doreen," he whispered, and turned and walked to his car, with Dozer following faithfully behind.

❧

For the first time since she began her business, Doreen regretted her decision to have her van painted to look like a moving billboard. She now wished that instead of the huge lumbering, brightly painted vehicle, she drove a Honda. Or a Mini. Anything small. And dingy neutral gray.

For the past week, Edwin had left his radio on during the day, but Mrs. Primline had informed him that their plan wasn't working. Dozer continued to howl to his heart's content.

At a loss for any better suggestions, Doreen didn't want to face anyone. Running to the front door, she hastily let herself in, hoping to be in and out faster than Mrs. Primline could make it across the street.

As she grabbed Dozer's collar to snap on the leash, Doreen froze. She could hear Edwin singing in the living room. She found it odd that he hadn't met her at the door, since Dozer put on his usual, dignified performance.

Edwin should have known she had arrived.

"Edwin?" she called from the entryway, then listened for his response. He continued singing, ignoring her. A bit off-key, but on the whole, he had a very pleasant voice. "Edwin, can you hear me?" she called, a little louder.

Obviously not. He kept singing. Why wasn't he at work? Doreen closed the door behind her and followed his voice into the living room. Edwin was nowhere to be seen. Instead, his voice was emanating from a car tape deck haphazardly attached by a tangle of wires to the back of the main stereo system.

Upon closer examination, she discovered it was an auto-reverse deck that Edwin had rigged to play continuously until someone hit the stop button.

She smiled at his ingenuity. Edwin had taped himself singing to his favorite songs and left it on for his dog to hear his beloved master's voice all day.

Instead of dreading being cornered by Mrs. Primline, Doreen now anticipated hearing if Edwin's plan worked. However, Mrs. Primline did not appear as she loaded Dozer into his kennel, and Doreen continued on her travels to pick up the rest of the dogs.

On the return trip, Mrs. Primline showed up with good news. She had not heard Dozer howl when Edwin left in the morning, and now the final test would tell if he howled when Doreen left. Mrs. Primline promised to tell Edwin the results as soon as he got home from work that evening.

❧

Edwin dragged his feet as he made his way inside. After a long day at work, he was tired and hungry and depressed. He had spent most of the day thinking about Doreen instead of concentrating on his job. Sure, he'd kissed her a few times, and she appeared to enjoy his company, and he didn't know where he would be in his spiritual journey if it wasn't for her, but overall, he didn't feel he was making any progress on a personal level. He wondered what he was doing wrong.

If it were any other woman, he knew a few ploys his single friends used when trying to snare a woman, but he wouldn't resort to tricks. Doreen was special, and she wasn't likely to fall for any phony moves. Besides, he wasn't going to pretend to be someone he was not. He loved her for her openness and honesty, and he wanted her to love him and want him the way he was.

Love? Since they had started seeing more of each other, Edwin found himself wondering what it would be like to come home to a person every day, instead of his dumb dog.

Not just any person. A woman. One woman. He wanted to come home to Doreen and a handful of kids.

Edwin shook his head. Love? Kids? Was he nuts? Getting old? He yawned and stretched his arms over his head. His friends would probably drag him somewhere for a psychiatric evaluation. They already thought he was deranged for going religious on them.

What could he do? He had tried charming her, he tried befriending her, he tried to impress her, he tried to humor her, he even trained his dog for her.

Edwin froze in mid-stretch. The only thing he hadn't done was pray for her. He'd done a fair amount of thanking God for putting her in his path, but he hadn't actually outright prayed for guidance to pursue the relationship. He parked himself on the couch. It seemed like a good place to start. He didn't want to wait until bedtime. And where was it written that you could only pray before you fell asleep, or in church? He seemed to remember Doreen discussing that with him on a number of occasions. It seemed Doreen was right again.

He lowered his face into his hands, and he prayed. He

prayed for guidance. He prayed for wisdom. He prayed for direction and insight. He prayed they would get to know each other better. What else could he do?

At his mumbled "amen," it came to him. Doreen had once made a comment about getting to know people by talking to friends and family. She appeared to be good friends with the older man at the pet store, Bill. He could simply strike up a conversation, and then casually ask about Doreen. She said he had known her since she was a kid, so maybe Bill could give him a few pointers and suggestions.

He checked his watch. This looked like a good time to practice heeling Dozer on the leash, and the round-trip to the pet store seemed like an ideal distance. He called Dozer, and hummed to himself the whole way to Pet Stuff.

He found the store deserted except for Bill. It was almost closing time, exactly like the day he met Doreen.

Tying Dozer securely to the bike rack, Edwin told him to stay, hoping for more permanent results than the last time.

Taking a deep breath to give himself a measure of courage, he entered the store. He tossed a handful of dog treats into a bag and sauntered casually to the counter, where Bill lazily paged through a supply catalog.

"Hi, Bill, how's it going?" he said cheerfully as he plunked the bag on the counter.

Bill looked at his face, then over his shoulder to the door. "Leave your dog outside?"

Edwin refused to take offense. The last time he was in here was probably the most embarrassing day of his life. "Yes, but this time he's fastened with one of your top-quality collars."

Bill mumbled something, then faced him. "Doreen with you?" he asked, again peering behind Edwin.

Edwin pulled at the collar of his shirt, which had suddenly gotten tighter. "Uh, no, I don't know where she is right now. Why do you ask?"

"Just wondering, Edwin, just wondering. She seems to be spending quite a bit of time with you lately, that's all." Bill gently balanced the bag on the scale, taking his sweet time, which was fine with Edwin.

"Tell me, Bill, you've known Doreen for a long time, haven't you?" Edwin pretended to be interested in a display of pet tags at the side of the counter, touching a few and turning them over to see both sides.

"Yup, since she was a little girl. Edna and I were good friends of her uncle before he died, and of course we've attended the same church for a couple of years."

"Ah," Edwin mumbled, trying to look interested as he examined a bone-shaped tag. "That's the uncle that left her the house and property out in the boonies, right?"

"Yup. Douglas McCullough. A good man."

Edwin had hoped Bill would be a little more talkative. "Does she ever see her cousins? Didn't anyone else want that private forest in the middle of nowhere?"

"Nope. No cousins. No brothers or sisters. No one but Doreen. He knew she'd put it to good use."

Edwin picked up another tag from the display, making it look like he couldn't decide on the color. "So, um, she's doing pretty good with her business, isn't she?"

Bill slowly punched a code into the scale, closed one eye, hit the clear button, then slowly and methodically checked the code list on the wall with one finger. "Sure is. I knew she could do it. Told her so, all the time."

Maybe Bill wasn't going to be as helpful as Edwin hoped for. "Good dog she's got. Good with the dogs, isn't she?"

"Gretchen's a good dog, well trained." Finding a number, Bill punched it in slowly, studied it, then hit the clear button again.

Edwin restrained himself from picking up the dog tags

and throwing them across the room. He smiled at Bill, transferring his attention to a box of rawhide chews. "We've been working on Dozer, and she's done wonders with him."

Ignoring the list, Bill picked up a book and started skimming through it. "Yup, good with dogs, nice girl, Doreen."

Edwin couldn't stand it anymore. Placing both palms on the counter, he stared Bill straight in the eye. He was about to shout that he wasn't there to talk about Doreen's dog when he noticed one of the corners of Bill's mouth quivering in an attempt not to laugh.

"Like her, don't you, Edwin?" asked Bill as he balanced himself on the stool behind the cash resister, tipping it onto two legs behind him.

"Yeah, and I wanted to ask you for some advice."

"Don't know how much help I'll be, but what do you want to know?"

"Do you think she likes me?" Edwin blurted out.

Bill smiled, and Edwin didn't know what to make of his expression. "I think you're a better judge of that than I. She probably does, or she wouldn't spend so much time with you."

Big help that was. "Well, what should I do?"

"Do?"

"I'm not sure how she feels about me. What should I do?"

Bill shrugged his shoulders. "Be yourself, be honest, and let her know how you feel. She might be just as nervous as you are." He pushed the bag of dog treats across the counter to Edwin, took Edwin's money, and placed a ripped plastic cover over the cash register.

Taking the hint, Edwin walked to the door with Bill trailing behind him. Bill flipped the sign to read "Closed," and Edwin heard the lock click behind him.

At least he'd had a nice walk.

twelve

Doreen set the hand brake as she stopped her van in Edwin's driveway. Every time she opened the door to his empty house and heard his tape-recorded voice singing songs of love and affection, it left her feeling melancholy.

At first, he sang strictly Top Forty songs, but lately he had switched to love ballads, or other songs promising undying love and devotion. It made her miss him, and she wondered if he thought of her during the day as often as she thought of him. *If I bought him a praise tape, maybe he would change his repertoire.*

Tomorrow was volleyball night, and she could hardly wait. He had promised to come and to wear shorts, claiming he had great legs. She had told him to let her be the judge of that. She remembered his slightly off-color reply, but laughed in spite of herself.

As she approached the front door, she saw it vibrate as Dozer thudded into it. She dreaded the day the dog actually hurt himself.

Beside the door, a newly planted rosebush looked suspiciously like Mrs. Primline's prize rose, the one she had dragged Edwin and Doreen into the backyard to see. Doreen fumbled with the keys, then dropped them as she remembered the time alone in Mrs. Primline's rose garden. With a sigh, she closed her eyes, shivering while she remembered the poignancy of his kiss. If she swallowed her pride and encouraged him a little, would he give her a repeat performance?

Dozer sat in the center of the entranceway, neither jumping nor running outside as she opened the door. In the short time she had been working with him, Dozer learned quickly what was expected of him, and now obediently waited for her command before he stepped outside. He couldn't hide his excitement, though, because his short stump of a tail wagged so hard it shook the entire dog.

Today, instead of rushing Dozer out to the van, Doreen rushed herself upstairs. Her consumption of coffee during her travels had caught up with her.

As she exited the washroom, Doreen could not help but notice the condition of the house. It was a total mess. In the washroom, one of the towels lay heaped on the floor and Edwin's razor and personal grooming items were strewn over the vanity. The kitchen was worse, with a tipped-over cereal box in the middle of the table, along with a dirty bowl and spoon, and the milk had been left out.

Hoping it could be saved, Doreen put it in the refrigerator. The counter was covered with crumbs where he had made himself a sandwich for lunch. The dirty knife and the carton of sandwich wrap were still on the counter, along with an open bread bag with the crusts still in it. Dirty dishes not only filled the sink, but lay in a disorganized mess on the counter as well. She fought the urge to clean up after him.

The condition of the living room was no better. The old tape player was hooked up and playing with wires sticking out everywhere, no change from the first day he installed his invention. Doreen had an eerie feeling of deja-vu as she stood alone in Edwin's house, listening to the sound of his less-than-melodious singing.

Doreen saw her old Bible sitting open on the couch; an unused bookmark lay on the arm less than a foot away. A half-empty coffee cup sat on the coffee table with no coaster beneath it, along with a plate surrounded by more crumbs than were on the plate itself. A crumpled shirt was draped over the armchair and one lone sock lay in the middle of the carpet, which needed vacuuming badly.

The man was a slob!

She had never seen the house in this condition. Doreen shook her head. She could imagine Edwin racing around the house putting things away before she got there. It was amazing she hadn't caught him the couple of times she arrived unannounced.

Doreen led Dozer out and locked the house, continuing on her way, thinking about Edwin all day long.

❧

Home again after delivering all the dogs to their respective homes, she immediately phoned Edwin's answering machine to leave a message that she might stop by for a visit after practice. She'd stopped at the Christian bookstore and bought him a praise tape, and intended to surprise him with it.

After a quick supper, Doreen changed and headed back into town for the weekly practice at the church.

A thought struck her as she unlocked the church door. Having been born and raised in a Christian home, she wondered what it must be like for Edwin to be starting his Christian walk as an adult. He openly admitted he had believed in God all his life, but what he now felt and discovered was very different. He'd entered into a whole new way of thinking, making progress one step at a time.

As expected, he fit right into her Tuesday Bible study, and from the many conversations with the group, was making good progress. A diligent reader, he was not ashamed to ask about anything he did not understand. He had also expressed interest in baptism. She'd almost cried in front of everyone.

The joy she experienced seeing his growth as a new Christian, however, only emphasized the lack of growth in their personal relationship. In a way, she almost resented his enthusiasm, because she felt a distant second. It made her feel both ashamed and selfish.

They talked long and often, sometimes about personal things, other times not, but their conversations always fell short of involvement. He never commented about missing her or seeing her again soon. After he had kissed her, twice, but who was counting, she had hoped for more of an indication, or at least some encouragement.

Doreen flicked the hidden switch to turn the lights on in the sanctuary, and stepped up to the glossy black grand piano. She opened the lid and keyboard cover, then tapped out a few chords before she sat on the bench. With no people in the room to dampen the sound, the piano had a strange echoing quality. The electric piano in the corner of her small living room at home did not produce the same effect.

She wanted to be alone in the large empty building this evening, so she had arrived well ahead of the scheduled practice time. She wanted to play alone, with no one listening but God. Could He help her sort out her relationship with Edwin?

For half an hour, she played some hymns as well as the more upbeat worship choruses, the music flowing from her heart and soothing her soul.

A voice at the end of a song caused her to jump. "Hi, Doreen. You're early."

It was Brad, the worship leader, who usually arrived first. Walking to her as she sat at the piano, he laid down his list of songs beside her music book.

"Hi, Brad. You scared me. I guess I wasn't watching the time."

"Hey, no problem. You sounded wonderful, as always. For a few minutes, I listened from the other side of the doorway. I think I'm going to change the lineup to include that last song."

Doreen smiled shyly. "You're the leader. You lead, I follow."

"Oh, brother!" he intoned sarcastically. "Don't give me any of that 'your wish is my command' stuff. Coming from you, of all people, I don't believe it."

"So, what's your point?" she asked, resisting the urge to stick her tongue out at him. She loved teasing Brad, and did it often.

"You always have more suggestions than any of the others."

"Me?"

"Don't start, Doreen." He wagged his finger at her.

Fortunately for her, the other members of the band chose that moment to walk in the door, and following a brief prayer, their practice was under way.

❧

By the time they finished, all Doreen could think of was her upcoming visit with Edwin. She practically ran to her van, and struggled to keep her speed to the legal limit on the short drive to his house.

Before she managed to knock, she heard the usual sound of Dozer slipping on the linoleum and sliding into the door with a thump. If he wasn't barking so much, she would have been worried that this time he finally managed to hurt himself.

Abruptly, the door opened, making her wonder if the thud this time had been Edwin bumping into the door.

"Hi!" he shouted in greeting above the volume of

Dozer's frantic barking. "Come on in!"

She raised her finger to tell him he no longer had to pull the dog back, that he sat just fine for her every day, but he had already closed the door and released the dog. She then raised one arm to shoulder height, and waited.

Edwin watched as Dozer walked, not ran, to Doreen, then sat quietly in front of her, his tail wagging a mile a minute beneath him, almost like he was waiting for her to do something. She touched his collar with one finger, and he stood, all four paws rooted to the floor. Doreen walked into the living room, but Dozer stayed put. When she made a single clap of her hands, Dozer turned and walked to her, sitting in front of her once more.

Edwin joined them in the living room and sat beside her on the couch. "How did you do that?" he asked.

She smiled sweetly at him, and his stomach clenched at the same time as his heart started to pound. "That's my signal before I attach the leash. He's to stay till we're ready to go to the van. Only I didn't go to the van this time." He noticed her eyes make a broad sweep of the living room as she ran one hand over his coffee table.

"Want a cup of coffee? I know it's late, so I made decaf."

When she nodded, Edwin stood, meaning to be the perfect host, to pour and bring it to her, but she followed him into the kitchen. He wondered what she was looking for, because again, her eyes ran a sweep of the entire room, including the drainboard, which was empty.

"Can I use your washroom?"

"You know you don't have to ask."

She smiled and nodded, then turned and left. Edwin poured her coffee, added the cream and sugar, pulled a couple of napkins out of the drawer, and carried a bag of donuts into the living room. Today he was glad he had checked his messages from work, which gave him the opportunity to stop on the way home to buy a treat for her.

She joined him on the couch, sitting primly, with her hands folded in her lap. If he didn't know any better, he would have thought she was planning something.

"I was here this afternoon."

"So? You're here every afternoon."

"I had to go upstairs to use your washroom. I hope you don't mind." She nibbled her bottom lip.

"Of course I don't mind. Why would I mind?"

Doreen smiled. "I see you've been busy."

Busy? The only thing he had done since he got home, donuts in hand, was run around like a madman cleaning up the house.

His mouth dropped, and his face paled. Edwin slumped and buried his face in his hands. Cleaning up the house! Now he understood. She had seen the disaster the house was in when she was here today. Doreen was a neat freak. He had tried hard since they met to keep the place tidy, but this last week he had let it slip while he made a couple of tapes for the dog, and things kind of got away from him.

The heat from his cheeks nearly burned his palms. He hoped she hadn't peeked inside his bedroom and seen the unmade bed or his underwear on the floor. Or a few days' worth of laundry piled up beside the closet door. "Oh, no," he moaned into his hands.

He flinched when her hand rested on his shoulder. "It's okay, Edwin, I'm just teasing you. Sometimes my house gets messy, too."

"Right." He shook his head, not removing his hands from his face. "I'll bet your house never gets *that* messy," he mumbled.

The pause felt like an eternity. "Well, maybe not that messy."

All he could do was groan.

"Hey, I bought you something."

His hands dropped to his lap. "You did?"

She reached for her purse, then pulled out a cassette tape and held it in the air. "Your neighbor said your method works, so I bought you some new material. Do you take requests?" She dropped the tape in his hand.

A picture of a clean-cut young man holding a guitar graced the cover. The name was unfamiliar. He turned it over to read the song titles. None of them was familiar either.

"It's my favorite praise tape. You might have heard a couple of the songs in church, but not recognized the names. I thought you might want to change your repertoire someday."

Edwin's ears burned, as well as his cheeks. On the first day of his experiment, he sang along to the first songs he touched that he half knew, just to see if it worked. When it did, he chose every love song he had in his CD collection, not for the stupid dog, but for Doreen. "I know it's bad, but it's worth the humiliation if it keeps the dog quiet."

"You have a lovely voice. With a little practice, I think you could be very good. Don't feel embarrassed. But I must admit that it's strange to hear your voice when you aren't home."

She thought he had a lovely voice? He thought he was terrible. "Really?" he asked.

"Really. It felt like I was intruding, walking around uninvited in your house, seeing signs of your presence all over the place when you weren't here."

Edwin waved his hands in front of him. "No, not that. Do you really like my singing?"

Doreen smiled. "Well, you could use a little practice, but you're not bad at all. And that's a special tape. If you play both channels you hear the singer and the music, but if you turn it all the way to one side, it only plays the music, so you can sing along to it like a solo performance. And knowing you didn't practice before you taped yourself, well, that's pretty good."

"Really?"

"Really."

"Should I be calling an agent?" He grinned broadly.

"Don't quit your day job."

He pretended to pout. Instead of responding, she stood and walked toward the front door. "I should go. You have to get up early tomorrow for work, and I have a long drive home yet. Tomorrow's volleyball night. Are you coming?"

Edwin followed her. "Wouldn't miss it." He crossed his arms over his chest. "Especially if Gary's going to be there."

He accompanied her to the van, chatting the entire time, as if he could draw out the time. Like a gentleman, he opened the door for her, then stood directly in front of her, as close as he could get without touching her. "Good night, Doreen. Glad you stopped by. And thanks for the tape."

"Good night, Edwin. You're welcome."

He rammed his hands in his pockets, more unsure of himself than ever before. At the touch of her fingers on his shoulder, he nearly jumped, but before he could figure out what she was doing, her lips brushed his cheek in a gentle peck, she clambered into her van, and slammed the door. The engine roared to a start, she waved to him from the other side of the closed window, and backed out of the driveway.

He couldn't even croak out a good-bye. Stiffly, he waved back, and watched her taillights shrink as she drove down the street and disappeared around the corner.

Did that really happen? He stuffed his hands back in his pockets and plodded back into the house. Maybe volleyball night held more promise than he thought.

thirteen

Doreen sat up with a jolt, blinking to focus her eyes in the darkness. The phone jangled beside the bed. As she groped for it, the blanket fell to her waist. The red light on the clock radio glowed 3:27 A.M. The only time people phoned in the middle of the night was when it was an emergency or a death. Her heart pounded.

"Hello?" she croaked.

"Doreen? It's Edwin." He stopped, the silence hung on the line.

Doreen gathered her wits. "Edwin? What's wrong?"

He cleared his throat, but his voice shook as he spoke. "I'm sorry to wake you up like this. My parents were in an accident this evening, and I'm calling from the hospital." His voice trembled. "I'm so sorry to call you in the middle of the night, but I need a friend to talk to."

Doreen's mind came together in a flash. "Are they. . . ?" Her voice trailed off. She couldn't finish the sentence.

"They've been in surgery all night. No one's told me anything. Doreen, I'm going crazy." Edwin cleared his throat, but didn't continue. In the background, a muffled voice called a doctor's name over the intercom, and the rumble of a cart being pushed down a corridor echoed through the phone.

"I'll be right there." She threw the blankets to the side and dangled her feet off the edge of the bed.

"Are you sure?"

"Yes, I'm sure. I'll be right there. Are you at General?"

His voice lowered in pitch, becoming husky. "Yes. Thanks."

Doreen threw on the first things she touched, splashed some cold water on her face, brushed her teeth, let the dog out, and was in the van in four minutes.

٭

At the emergency reception area, a nurse led her to the room where Edwin waited. One look at him, and Doreen's heart wrenched.

He sat slumped in a chair with his face in his hands. On the table beside him were eight or so Styrofoam coffee cups with the edges picked ragged, pieces of white foam chips strewn everywhere. Instead of his normally straight and confident posture, his shoulders hunched in defeat as he sat in misery.

He looked pitiful and alone.

As the nurse left, Doreen silently crossed the room to stand in front of him. When she gently placed her hand on his shoulder, he flinched nervously and raised his head. Dark circles shadowed his eyes, and his face was drawn and pale. Doreen feared the worst.

As soon as he laid eyes on her, Edwin reached out to Doreen and pulled her into a tight embrace. Leaning his face into her stomach as she remained standing, he drew a ragged sigh.

"Thanks for coming." His voice was soft, but hoarse, the stress of the night apparent in his shaking hands.

Doreen stroked his soft hair as a means of comfort, discovering it messy and tangled, probably from running his hands through it hundreds of times throughout the strain of the evening. "How are you?"

"I gave blood earlier, and I don't feel so good. I think I could throw up."

She studied the mass of empty coffee cups. That much bad hospital coffee would have been enough to turn anyone's stomach. Having donated blood before, she knew it could leave a person feeling queasy. They would have given him a glass of juice and a cookie afterward, but she also knew he wouldn't have eaten since supper time, which was over ten hours ago. Between the coffee, giving blood, hunger, and all the stress, no wonder he felt ill.

"I've got a granola bar in my purse. Do you want it?"

He shook his head, his forehead still pressed tight against her stomach.

"Any word?" she whispered.

He shook his head again, his grip tightening behind her back. Edwin drew a deep breath and held her like a drowning man clinging for dear life before he finally went under. "No, but they're not optimistic. Last I heard was over an hour ago, they're both still in surgery. Neither my mom or dad is expected to make it. But no one's come with any bad news yet."

"Oh, Edwin. . ." She ran the fingers of both hands into his hair and rubbed her thumbs against his temples. She didn't know what else to do but let him talk.

"The police have witnesses who saw the other car run a red light at a high speed and hit them broadside, sending them into oncoming traffic, right into a dump truck." Edwin stopped to draw a shuddering breath. "Doreen, the other driver was drunk. He walked away, and my mom and dad are going to die." His shoulders heaved as he started to sob.

Her hands left his hair and slipped onto his shoulders. Tears stung her own eyes as she listened to his outpouring of emotion, but she choked them back. He needed her to be strong for him, making her doubly grateful that she could be there for him. She couldn't imagine how horrible it must have been for him to be alone so long in the cold sterile atmosphere of the hospital, waiting for an outcome that didn't have much hope.

"Why?" he sobbed. "Why them? Why did this have to happen? If they die, it will be for nothing."

Doreen's heart was breaking for him. "I don't know, I wish I had the answers, but I don't. And I wish there was something I could say or do for you, but the best thing I can do is pray."

He nodded into her stomach and gulped for breath. "I'd like that. I'm new at this, and really don't know what to say."

With difficulty, she composed her thoughts. A few days ago she had told him that no magic formula existed to make God give you what you want, no matter how important or necessary you thought it was. Sometimes bad things happened to good people, and there was nothing anyone could do. Only God could make a miracle happen.

Doreen sucked in a deep breath as she pried herself loose. Edwin lifted the bottom of his T-shirt and wiped his face on it. Rather than stare at him as he collected himself, Doreen gave him time to regain his composure. She sat in the chair beside him as she dug in her purse for a tissue, and handed him the granola bar at the same time. He stared at it like it was a foreign substance, but ate it anyway, and stuffed the wrapper inside one of the many shredded cups.

"Let's pray now. Just tell God how you feel, ask him for what you want. It's okay to beg, whatever you're feeling in your heart. You don't have to say anything out loud. Go ahead, Edwin, talk to God. He hears your thoughts, whatever they are."

Angling herself toward him, she grasped both his hands, but he pulled his fingers out of hers, shifted closer until they sat side by side and embraced her fully, resting his forehead on her shoulder. "I need to hold you close, Doreen, to feel you breathe, and feel your warmth. I feel like a part of me has been ripped away."

She nodded, then rested her head against his. Alone together, the room silent except for the typical hospital background noise, she felt rather than heard his ragged breathing, released in sporadic sighs as he prayed in his own way. Doreen prayed in silence with him, grateful to be able to share this private moment in God's presence with him. She offered up her own prayers, not only for Edwin's strength and peace, but for the recovery of his parents, praying for the miracle that would save them.

Holding him tight, she felt his breathing become more even as he continued to pray silently. How she loved him at that moment. She deeply yearned for something to strengthen and console him, but all she could think of was to hold him to offer him comfort. She rubbed circles on his back, and he sighed, gave her a gentle squeeze, but otherwise didn't move.

As she continued to hold him, Edwin became more relaxed, and the more relaxed, the heavier he got. She continued to rub soothing circles as the time dragged. The clock on the wall neared seven, and Doreen knew in half an hour Edwin should be arriving at work, which of course he was in no condition to do. It had been a while since they spoke, and although she didn't want to disturb him, she had to move. Edwin was squashing the breath out of her.

"Edwin?" she whispered softly, but he didn't respond. "Edwin?"

His arms slowly floated down, sinking to rest on the chair behind her back. He was asleep. Thoroughly exhausted, after being awake for over twenty-four hours, the trauma and stress had taken its toll.

Gently, Doreen cradled his head with one hand and the center of his shoulders with the other, and lowered him as gently as his weight would allow. Once she had him lying across the chairs, she lifted his legs up until he lay flat along the row. He covered five chairs.

She couldn't help herself. Doreen sat in the chair nearest his head and watched him sleep. Unable to stop herself, she gently caressed his cheek, feeling the scratchy stubble of his beard against the softness of her palm. It pained her to see him so helpless. Even fast asleep and completely relaxed, his face showed the strain of the night, and she closed her eyes in a short prayer for good news when he awoke.

To pass the time, she leaned back in her chair, rested her feet up on the chair across from her, and picked up an old magazine from the table. Before long, the words became a blur, and as her eyes got heavier and heavier, her head slumped forward. A slight noise in the hall brought her eyes open as her head jerked up with a start.

She checked her watch. In ten minutes, Edwin was due to arrive at his job. She turned her head. He hadn't moved a muscle.

She decided to call his boss to explain Edwin's absence and walked into the hall to use the pay phone. Even if they heard good news, he still wouldn't be in any condition to go to work. She swallowed, hoping the news would be good as she paged through the phone book, looking for the name of the courier company where he worked.

The receptionist answered on the first ring, making Doreen realize she had not rehearsed what she was going to say. "I'm calling for Edwin Olson, he won't be in today, and I was wondering if you would connect me with the right person."

"That would be Mr. Randolph. One moment." With a click and a ring, she waited.

"Randolph," a male voice answered sharply.

"I'm calling for Edwin Olson," Doreen repeated meekly. "He won't be in to work today."

For a few seconds, the man remained silent as he contemplated her message. "Who is this?" he asked. "Wait, let me guess, you're Doreen. Has something happened to Edwin?"

She wondered how Edwin's boss knew her name. "No," she stammered, "he's okay, but his parents were in a car accident yesterday evening, and he's been at the hospital all night. He's just fallen asleep now. I was wondering if it was all right if he didn't come in today."

Mr. Randolph paused. "How bad is it?" Doreen strained the phone cord to peek back at Edwin, still flaked out, sprawled across the hard, vinyl chairs. One arm now rested across his face over his eyes.

She didn't know how much information it was proper to give him, but decided to go with the complete truth. "Both his parents were in a car accident. They've been in surgery all night, and I've been told it doesn't look good. We haven't heard the results yet, so I, uh, I'm not too hopeful. . ." Doreen gulped and let her voice trail off. Squeezing her eyes shut, she dreaded the outcome, once again praying for a miracle.

"Tell him to take all the time off he needs, and keep me up-to-date. And tell him I'll be praying for him and his family."

Doreen opened her mouth, but no sound came out. A click echoed in her ear, so she hung up the phone and returned to Edwin, still sleeping, sprawled out on the hard vinyl chairs.

Now that Edwin's job had been taken care of, what about hers? Bill had said once that he could fill in for her in case of emergency. The situation with Edwin's parents didn't directly affect her. Nevertheless, it seemed heartless to leave Edwin alone while his parents' lives hung in the balance.

She stood watching Edwin sleeping as she battled with her decision. She couldn't leave without telling him, but neither did she want to wake him to tell him she was deserting him to go about her business. When he said he needed her, she came, and she intended to see him through to the conclusion of the crisis, no matter what the outcome.

She walked back to the phone to call Bill. As she was dialing the first digit, a doctor walked past her and into the waiting room. With a start, her heart skipped a beat, she fumbled the phone, hung up, and ran to be beside Edwin.

"Mr. Olson?" the doctor said gently, standing beside Edwin's prone form.

At the sound of his name, Edwin woke with a start. He jerked to an upright position, then blinked repeatedly as he swayed, probably from sitting up too fast. Doreen pressed one hand onto his shoulder to keep him seated. That was all he needed, if he passed out on top of everything else. She gave his shoulder a gentle squeeze.

With a pounding heart, part dreading and part anticipating the news, Doreen held her breath.

Edwin was shaking. His heartbeat raced as the fog in his head cleared. His legs trembled so badly he was afraid to stand. Feeling Doreen's gentle grip on his shoulder gave him the strength he needed to hear the report, whatever it might be. He placed one hand over Doreen's on his left shoulder and waited.

"Yes?" Edwin gulped, almost choking on the tightness in his throat.

The surgeon held his gloves with one hand and ran his other hand over his hair, pushing it off his forehead. "They're both stable. So far, so good," he said gravely, pausing to allow his statement to sink in.

Edwin could see from the surgeon's face and tone of voice that the ordeal was far from over for his parents.

"But?" he asked, clearing his throat.

The surgeon looked at him with a tired smile. "But it's been a rough surgery for both of them, and it's going to be a long recovery, but with the proper rest and care, both of them should make a complete recovery."

Edwin squeezed his eyes tightly shut. "Thank you," he whispered hoarsely. With his eyes open, he stood to face the surgeon on shaky legs. "Thank you so much. When can I see them?"

The surgeon nodded wearily, signs of wear from all-night surgery evident on his face. "Both of them are still under heavy sedation, and you can only see them for five minutes. The nurse will take you." He turned and left the room.

A nurse now beckoned them from the doorway. "This way," she said as she smiled, holding out one hand as a signal for them to follow her.

Edwin grasped Doreen's hand, then let go. Turning to the nurse, he lifted one finger, signaling to her that he would be a few seconds. "You don't have to see this," he said quietly. "I'm not sure what to expect, but I'm sure it won't be a pretty sight, and you don't know them. You don't have to come with me, you can wait here, or go home if you want."

Doreen looked up at him, then reached out to hold one of his hands with both of hers. "If you want, I'll go with you."

Edwin squeezed his eyes shut. He'd never loved her more. He wanted to tell her that, but this was neither the time nor the place. He returned the gentle squeeze. "I'd like that. Thank you."

Together, they turned to follow the nurse to the intensive care ward, hand in hand. Heavily sedated, his parents lay in beds side by side, tubes and wires taped to them, monitors beeping, lights flashing. Looking at them this way made him feel physically sick, but he was so grateful they were alive that tears stung his eyes. A tear trickled out when he closed his eyes briefly for a short prayer of thanks. He swiped at his face with his forearm.

"I'm sorry, but you have to leave now." The nurse reappeared, and escorted them out.

Edwin stared unseeing at the entrance to the ward, his mind blank.

"I'll drive you home. We can pick your car up tonight."

Wearily, Edwin nodded and followed Doreen to the parking lot. Physically and emotionally drained, he still managed to be content. If this had happened a month ago, he could picture himself pacing and swearing and punching holes in the walls at the injustice of it all. Instead, he felt at peace that his parents were alive, and the woman he loved was at his side.

Climbing up into the van, Edwin realized this was the first time he had actually been inside of it, so he decided to check it out. Dog kennels lined the walls in neat rows, securely fastened to a framework which kept them safely stacked and accessible. A bin for leashes, a water container, and a fan were also securely bolted down for safe transport, as well as an air-conditioning unit mounted on the roof of the van.

He grinned. "Very nice outfit. I wish I was one of your charges."

"You old dog, you," Doreen chided him.

Edwin stared out the window the entire trip home. No matter how hard he tried to concentrate, he couldn't think.

He had to blink to get his brain in gear when she pulled into his driveway.

"Don't worry about my car, I'll take a cab when I wake up. I know you're busy today, and you'll want to go straight to sleep when you're done."

The second he opened the door and stepped out, he could hear Dozer's wild barking from inside. "I didn't have the tape on, I wonder if he howled like he does when I go to. . ." His voice trailed off. He clamped his eyes shut, stiffened his back, and slapped his palm to his forehead. "Work! I was supposed to be at work an hour ago!"

Placing a hand on his shoulder, Doreen shook her head.

"No, I phoned in for you. I spoke to a Mr. Randolph and told him what happened. He said to take as much time off as you need, but he does want you to keep him informed. And he said—"

Without waiting for her to finish, Edwin grabbed Doreen, pulling her into a tight embrace, burying his face in her hair. At first, she was rigid, but she immediately softened, and leaned into him. "Thanks for everything, I don't know what I would have done without you. Not only today, but every day. You've made such a difference in my life, you're my very best friend."

Not giving her a chance to resist, Edwin lowered his mouth to hers and kissed her hotly and desperately with all the love in his heart. The single reason he stopped kissing her and let her go was to avoid putting on a show in front of the neighbors. With that thought in mind, he reluctantly released her.

"See you tomorrow." He gently kissed her again, turned, and retreated into his house.

fourteen

Saturday. Dog obedience day. Doreen's favorite day.

After sleeping through volleyball night, she suspected Edwin had done the same, since he did not phone Friday evening. Now she missed him all the more. She glanced up at the clock, wondering why he still hadn't called. Usually, by this time on a Saturday morning, he not only would have phoned to invite himself over, he would already be knocking on her door.

Doreen wondered whether she should phone to confirm he was coming. She refused to let her mind wander to the possibility that something had gone wrong with his parents. And certainly after kissing her the way he had when she dropped him off from the hospital there would be no hesitation or question of his welcome.

Receiving no answer, Doreen did not leave a message on his answering machine, not knowing what to say.

She tapped her foot, then started to pace. It was past the time of his usual arrival. Visiting hours at the hospital weren't until afternoon. Where was he? The butterflies in Doreen's stomach shifted into overdrive.

In answer to her question, Gretchen started running in circles and barking, then leapt out the doggie door. Usually when someone arrived, including Edwin, Gretchen instinctively waited inside the house to protect her. Doreen's nerves were suddenly on edge.

With a shove, she banged the door open to see Dozer, running all alone down her long driveway, with no sight of

163

Edwin or his car.

The two dogs gleefully jumped in circles at each other, then ran toward her. Gretchen and Dozer whizzed past Doreen into the house. Where was Edwin?

Doreen walked anxiously down the driveway. Unless something serious had happened, Edwin would not allow his precious dog to run off.

Doreen ran to the end of her long driveway. Panting now, she looked down the street and spotted his car pulled over to the side of the road, by itself, with no apparent damage. Edwin was nowhere to be seen.

As she jogged toward the car, she saw Edwin's head appear from behind the open trunk. He moved awkwardly along the side of the car, bent at the waist, sleeves pushed up to his elbows, rolling a tire.

Heaving a sigh of relief, Doreen slowed her pace to a fast walk, soon arriving at Edwin's side. He grunted and muttered something under his breath as he struggled to remove the lug nuts.

"Problems?" she asked.

"Huh?" He raised his head, smiled at her, then lowered it again. "Oh. Hi. Yeah," grunted Edwin as he pried off the flat tire and heaved the spare into place. "Looks like I ran over a big hunk of something metal on the road, and it shredded the tire instantly."

Doreen examined the destroyed tire that was leaning on the side of the car. From the appearance of the shredded rubber, Edwin was lucky it had not been more serious.

"Need some help?"

Edwin mumbled as he tightened the last lug nut. "Nope. Got it." He tossed the remains of his tire into the trunk and wiped his hands on the front of his pants. "Do you know you have wild animals out here?"

"Wild animals?" Deer lived in the woods, although they were seldom seen near the road, and of course often the raccoons could be pesky at night, but she'd never seen anything that could be termed a "wild animal."

He grinned as he examined his hands, then slapped them together, as if that would remove the dirt that couldn't be wiped on his pants. "Yeah, Dozer and I saw these monster squirrels running in the trees. You should have seen him go after those killers."

"I'll bet."

With complete disregard for anything else he might have had in the trunk, Edwin tossed his tools and the jack on top of the ruined tire, then slapped his thighs to get the dust out. "Let's go. Hop in."

Doreen smiled. He had inadvertently smeared some grime on his cheek and across the bridge of his nose. She didn't mention it, waiting for them to get back to her house so she could do it properly.

"How are your parents?" Doreen asked hesitantly.

Edwin sat in the driver's seat, placed his hands on the steering wheel, and turned to face her. "Visiting hours aren't until afternoon, but I phoned and they said they're as well as can be expected. I guess that's good news."

Judging by the expression on his face, he was still very worried. "Yes, I think it is."

"Dozer make it okay to your place?" he asked as he started the engine and pulled onto the road.

"Yes. After all, I'm here, aren't I? But I'd really like to know why you let him go."

Edwin laughed lamely and shrugged his shoulders. "He was driving me nuts. He knew where we were going, and he was so excited, I just let him go ahead of me. He brought you, didn't he?"

She nodded. The dogs both popped out the doggie door when the car arrived beside the house. "I was worried when your dog showed up without you."

"Sorry about that. I would have tied a note to his collar, but I didn't have a pen."

Doreen excused herself to visit the washroom, and when she returned, she found Edwin in the kitchen washing his hands with her dish detergent. He found a clean spot on his pants to wipe them, helped himself to a large glass of water and stood at the sink as he noisily glugged it down, then choked when he saw her standing in the doorway.

"You startled me, I didn't see you." One eye narrowed. "What have you got in your hand?"

Doreen held out a wet facecloth. "What's that for?" he asked, rechecking his hands, making sure they were clean.

"You have dirt on your face. Sit down. Look up."

Doreen stood in front of him as he sat in the chair. Edwin closed his eyes and sighed as she wound her fingers into his hair to steady his head while she used the warm cloth to wipe the dirt smudges off his cheek and nose.

"Mmm. I like this," he mumbled.

"What?" Doreen asked absently, wiping away the last black remnants.

Edwin kept his eyes closed as he leaned into her hand. "This. You."

The cloth stopped moving, then resumed motion. Like? If that was the best he could do, then she would take it. Yesterday she was in the best friend category, whatever that meant. She supposed one had to "like" their best friend, although the ranking still managed to disappoint.

But what could she expect? Up till now, she had never given Edwin any indication of how she felt about him, or ever encouraged him in any way, except for a few stolen kisses she wouldn't forget till her dying day. For the most part, she'd purposely kept her distance, trying not to mix helping him in his Christian discovery with anything personal.

Since he started it, even if all he said was "I like you," she could at least do the same. If he didn't respond, then at least she would know where she stood. The thought terrified her.

She continued to wipe at a spot that had long since been wiped clean, justifying the ministrations with the knowledge that he was enjoying it.

"I like you, too." She gulped. Was that the best she could come out with? This baring your soul stuff wasn't going to be as easy as she thought.

Edwin opened his eyes to watch Doreen. While unexpectedly overjoyed to hear her admit that much, he wondered what brought it on. His heart started to beat faster. Saying out loud that she liked him was the best admission she'd given so far. Was there more? Could there be more?

Edwin wiped his sweaty palms on his pants. "You know what I'd like?"

Doreen swallowed hard, opened her eyes wide, and stared at him. "What?" Her voice sounded too shrill.

Edwin sucked in a deep breath to summon his courage. He might as well go all the way. "I'd like to get married."

"What?" she choked out.

"To you." Edwin grabbed her by the waist and pulled her into his lap while he figured she would still be pliant enough to go. "I want to be married to you, Doreen."

In the blink of an eye, Doreen found herself in Edwin's lap. She trembled all over as his fingertips trailed slowly up her arm, up her neck, then over her cheek until they rested on her lips. "This better not be some kind of joke," she said, recalling the unpleasant scene the last time he mentioned marriage. Her voice quivered as she continued. "I mean it, Edwin."

"I love you, Doreen."

The expression on his face was a mixture of fear and anticipation. Doreen blushed and struggled to maintain eye contact.

"I love you, too, Edwin."

Two fingers rubbed her lower lip, then both hands rested on the nape of her neck as he drew her mouth to his for a long, slow kiss.

Doreen's eyes remained closed for a few moments after they separated. How had they gone from wiping a few smudges off his nose to declarations of love and marriage?

Doreen's mind nearly spun out of control. Even though he continually phoned to invite himself over, she had no idea that he felt this way. The thought hit her like a ton of bricks.

What would marriage to Edwin mean? What would he be like to live with? A bit of a scatterbrain and more than a bit of a slob, he was undisciplined and his attitude too offhanded. No doubt some things about her drove him nuts too, but what was wrong with that? That was all part of what made Edwin who he was, and that was who she had fallen in love with.

What about his relationship with God? He was a new believer, but she was certain that his decision had been genuine. They both had a lot of growing still to do, but she was confident that he would love her as God directed, in faith, trust, fidelity, and with all the love in his heart. She cleared her throat and reached out to touch his cheek, all her love for him as obvious as the stars in her eyes. "What about being friends, like you said yesterday?"

He held the hand touching his cheek with his, leaned his face into it, then kissed her palm. Her breath caught as shivers ran all through her body to her toes. With the other hand he reached down to the small of her back to steady her as she remained seated in his lap. "Don't you think it's important to be best friends when you're married?"

Doreen's heart leapt into double-time at that thought. "You've mentioned marriage before. Why should I take you seriously this time?"

Regret shadowed his face. "You know, I meant it when I said I thought we should get married, but I was so nervous I tried to joke about it when I shouldn't have. I can only say again that I'm sorry. I didn't mean to hurt you, Doreen. I wish I could make it up to you."

Unable to look her in the face, Edwin closed his eyes and kissed her palm once more, then her wrist, as a show of apology.

Her heart pounded in her chest and she forced herself to breathe again. "And I'm sorry I overreacted. I don't know what made me jump down your throat like that. I'm really sorry, too."

Still concentrating on her hand, Edwin swallowed, dropping his voice to a whisper. "Enough sorrys. I do want to get married, because I love you with all my heart and all my soul and all my mind. I want to marry you before God, and love you as my best friend and my wife, just like I read in Corinthians." He turned his face up to hers. "That was really beautiful, and I want us to love each other, like that, forever. Doreen, will you marry me?"

Touched by his tender and solemn words, tears of joy silently streamed down Doreen's face. Not wanting to break into sobs, she bit her quivering bottom lip.

Gently, Edwin reached up to wipe away her tears with

his fingers. "Aw, Doreen, please don't cry. I didn't mean to make you sad, I want to make you happy."

"Oh, Edwin," she gulped indelicately, "you have. I want to marry you, too. I think we will be very happy together."

Slipping his fingers from her cheek, Edwin drew her closer for a long kiss.

Edwin released her mouth only long enough to catch his breath. "I love you, Doreen," he sighed, lowering his mouth to Doreen's again.

"I love you, too, Edwin," she whispered hoarsely, waiting.

"We're going to be very, very happy."

"Yes, Edwin, we are."

A Letter To Our Readers

Dear Reader:

In order that we might better contribute to your reading enjoyment, we would appreciate your taking a few minutes to respond to the following questions. When completed, please return to the following:

Rebecca Germany, Managing Editor
Heartsong Presents
PO Box 719
Uhrichsville, Ohio 44683

1. Did you enjoy reading *Walking the Dog?*
   ❏ Very much. I would like to see more books
      by this author!
   ❏ Moderately
      I would have enjoyed it more if _____

   _____

2. Are you a member of **Heartsong Presents**? ❏Yes ❏No
   If no, where did you purchase this book?_____

   _____

3. What influenced your decision to purchase this
   book? (Check those that apply.)

   ❏ Cover   ❏ Back cover copy

   ❏ Title   ❏ Friends

   ❏ Publicity   ❏ Other_____

4. How would you rate, on a scale from 1 (poor) to 5
   (superior), the cover design?_____

5. On a scale from 1 (poor) to 10 (superior), please rate the following elements.

___Heroine   ___Plot

___Hero   ___Inspirational theme

___Setting   ___Secondary characters

6. What settings would you like to see covered in **Heartsong Presents** books?_____

_____

_____

7. What are some inspirational themes you would like to see treated in future books?_____

_____

_____

8. Would you be interested in reading other **Heartsong Presents** titles?   ❏ Yes   ❏ No

9. Please check your age range:
   ❏ Under 18   ❏ 18-24   ❏ 25-34
   ❏ 35-45   ❏ 46-55   ❏ Over 55

10. How many hours per week do you read? _____

Name _____

Occupation_____

Address_____

City_____ State_____ Zip _____

A Romantic Collection
of Inspirational Novellas

Discover how two words, so softly spoken, create one glorious life with love's bonds unbroken. *I Do,* a collection of four all-new contemporary novellas from **Heartsong Presents** authors, will be available in May 1998. What better way to love than with this collection written especially for those who adore weddings. The book includes *Speak Now or Forever Hold Your Peace* by Veda Boyd Jones, *Once Upon a Dream* by Sally Laity, *Something Old, Something New* by Yvonne Lehman, and *Wrong Church, Wrong Wedding* by Loree Lough. These authors have practically become household names to romance readers, and this collection includes their photos and biographies. (352 pages, Paperbound, 5" x 8")

Heart♥ng

HEARTSONG PRESENTS *TITLES AVAILABLE NOW:*

(If ordering from this page, please remember to include it with the order form.)

·········· Presents ··········

Great Inspirational Romance at a Great Price!

Heartsong Presents books are inspirational romances in contemporary and historical settings, designed to give you an enjoyable, spirit-lifting reading experience. You can choose wonderfully written titles from some of today's best authors like Veda Boyd Jones, Yvonne Lehman, Tracie Peterson, Nancy N. Rue, and many others.

When ordering quantities less than twelve, above titles are $2.95 each.
Not all titles may be available at time of order.